Wind Walker

Wind Walker

Wind Walker Series: Book I

Charlie Barker

Wind Walker by Charlie Barker
Published by Tiny Studio 92

Editor: Carol Barker

Cover Artwork by Jonas G.
Instagram.com/jonasg.artist

Cover Layout by Charlie Barker

ISBN-13: 9798551732839

Table of Contents

PROLOGUE

Our conversation ends abruptly as we near the house. Something isn't right. I can't quite put a finger on it. I realize that I've slowed down. Ari is half a stride in front of me. I place my hand on her shoulder and we stop. Immediately, seeing my face in her rear view, she understands that something is wrong; but she doesn't know what it is either. Is it the sound? Yes, the sound. Pods are very quiet, but they do make a minimal amount of noise. One must have pulled up at the front of the house. Maybe several based on the low hum I hear. I sign as much to Ari. We can see the house. It's only 100 meters away. The vastness of the forest hides us from anyone who would give a cursory scan. I increase the opacity on my video feeds just a little bit. I don't want to miss any movement behind me. The back door of the house opens and I see Father walk outside with a Patrician.

"Elias, Elias, wherefore art thou?" He's nearly yelling, addressing the forest at large, "Betwixt the brevities of life we must eat, and the servants have preparethed the food."

We come back at exactly the same time every day. Father knows this very well. He's specifically telling us not to come home.

"We should fight," I sign.

Ari turns slightly so I can see her hands, remaining focused on the house. "How many Patricians are there?"

I don't know. She doesn't know. It's the obvious question.

"Five…yes, fight," she continues. "Ten? Maybe. More? Definitely not."

"I think there's several pods out front, and they're looking for us now. At minimum there would be four, one for each of us. But it's likely there's eight or more."

"We can't, Eli. I know you want to, but we can't. If they find out you're of August, we're all dead. If they find out your family has been educating me, we're all dead. If they see us shift the wind…we're not wind walkers, but I can't imagine they would be pleased to find out we can lay waste to a room full of armed men with the wave of an arm. Even if we escaped they would hunt us."

My heart is racing. I can barely breath. Everything in me wants to scream and fight, but I am not allowed. I see Father turn to the Patrician, voice still blaring above the soft hum of the pods. "Do you hear that, sir? The silence, it calls to me. The vast emptiness of the forest receives my voice and I doth go forth into it as it calls me with silence." It's all complete nonsense, at least to the Patrician who is becoming visibly angry even from our vantage point 100 meters away. But the message Father gives us is exactly what we need: leave for Evanwood and the Silent Order. This is it. We are never going home again. Have we been beaten already? Certainly, if we stay. We have to go. Now.

CHAPTER 1
ELI

Nine months in a sealed chamber, fluid filling my lungs and a feeding tube attached directly to my stomach; this would be a great model for extended space flight...if such a thing were actually possible. I don't understand how I have come to be here—on Merced—but I am here nevertheless. There's a strange feeling; the gravity here is a little less than Earth's. Not enough to make a real difference, but it feels off; like when a plane dips for half a second—that falling feeling—that's how I feel. Every time I move an arm and return to motionless I expect a little more pressure, but I find lightness. It's going away though. I won't remember it soon. That's not right. I'll remember that it *was* different, but I'll forget how it felt. The difference is small and only for a moment. It's fleeting—a strange sensation. I bet I could jump an inch or two higher; although I can't really jump right now, can I?

Time to test out another sense. Is feeling gravity a sense? Must be. Either way, time to open my eyes. Bright! I don't like it! Shut them, shut them now! That feels better, but what did I see? Light, a lot of light; also people, or at least people shaped blurs. My eyes must not be very good yet, but that's to be expected. What about my skin? I can feel the air. It hurts. Why does the air hurt? Rage! I've never felt such rage before. I muffle a scream and control myself. Still angry. No one told me it would feel like this. To be fair, no one has really told me anything up to this point. I've heard them speak, but not to me. I guess I've been inaccessible so far. Someone is wrapping a blanket around me. Ahhh...so much better. Warm. Calm. Sleep.

***

Everything is a blur. My eyesight is literally awful. I'm not even sure how many days I've been here. I sleep a lot. I'm awake now. I'm laying in a bassinet two rooms away, but I can still hear Mother and Father discussing whether or not they should check on me. It's so much easier to understand everything without fluid in my ears.

"Isaac, he never cries!"

"He's just content, Euny; there is nothing wrong with him."

"Maybe we should check on him."

"Maybe we should just let him sleep."

"But I also just want to see him. I miss him!"

"Euny, it's only been two hours!"

"Doesn't mean I can't miss him. If *only* you loved our child as much as I do, then you might know the pain I feel when I haven't seen his face for two hours."

"Do you get dizzy when you spin your words that fast"

"Just a little." The smirk on her face is audible. "I'm going to check on him now."

I let out a little cry before she opens the door, just to ease her conscience. She's in. Ok, stop crying and smile.

"Isaac, he's smiling!"

"It's probably just gas," Father hollers from the other room. "Babies don't smile for at least a month. He's only a week old."

There it is: seven days...feels like longer. Wait, what did he say? Babies don't smile. I forgot, babies don't smile! Time to scrunch my face and push as hard as I can. The tiniest toot sounds off from down under.

Mother's tone is playful and defeated as she calls out, "You were right, it was just gas." She turns to me and speaks softly, "But you are just perfect in every way."

Mother holds me and sings to me. It's the only thing I want to hear; her voice is perfect. It soothes like nothing I've ever known before. Soft, sweet, colorful. She must be tired—I've seen what childbirth inflicts on a body—but she never complains. She even *tries* to do housework. She's carrying me into another room with the intent to clean right now; determination set in her eyes. But I've seen this play out half a dozen times already...it doesn't end well for her.

She moves to the center of the room. There's nothing in front of her to clean. She turns, turns again and turns again. There's nothing to clean. With each turn her brow becomes more and more furrowed. She swears under her breath and marches into another room.

"Isaac, I am *not* an invalid."

"I would never suggest such a thing, my dear. I just want you to rest and enjoy this perfect moment in our lives."

"You say that every time," she groans.

"Fine, how about you give me the baby and you can be free to scour the house for something to clean."

Begrudgingly, mother hands me to father and walks towards the kitchen.

"I'm gonna tell you a secret, little buddy," Father whispers to me. "I already cleaned the kitchen. But let's just keep that between you and me."

After a few moments Mother's frustrated growl emanates from the kitchen as she discovers what I have just learned. She glares at Father as she passes by, then mutters to herself as she climbs the stairs, "Fine! You think you're going to take care of everything? I'll show you!"

Father's face is beaming as he gets up and walks with me to the base of the stairs. Still smiling, he looks down at me. "She's gonna be so mad! But she's very tired and deserves a bit of a rest."

"Are you serious?" She yells from upstairs. "You made the bed too?"

"I just thought you might like to take a nap. There's nothing like crawling into a freshly made bed, and you've been working so hard with the baby."

"I'm going to take a nap because *I* want to, having nothing to do with your shenanigans! And you better believe that when I get up I *will* find some housework to do!"

A nap does sound good. I'll just shut my eyes…

***

It's been a few weeks since I arrived here. I have come to decide that I live in a tree house. This is my hypothesis. This is not to be confused with a treehouse; disambiguation is key here. I don't live inside a house that is suspended in a tree; I live *in* a tree...at least as far as I can tell. I wish my vision were better, but hopefully I can get a closer look at some things today...for science, of course.

Squirming in Father's arms while flailing my own has the intended effect. He lays me down on the floor so I can play. I'm on my belly. Perfect. First things first, give in to my insatiable urge to lick the floor. I know it's gross, but this is science, and I might as well indulge my baser instincts in the name of science. It tastes like wood—no surprise there. I can feel the grain. Move and check again. This is the dumbest thing I have ever done, but living in a tree house would be supremely cool, so I must labor on.

Are there any seams in the wood? No, none. Over the course of a few minutes, using my belly as a fulcrum, I manage to turn 180 degrees. Still, no seams anywhere to be seen. As far as I can tell, the floor of the house is one solid piece of wood.

Father rises from his chair. "Now don't you go anywhere you little munchkin," he says, wagging a finger at me.

I couldn't have planned this better. The moment he leaves the room is my time. Deep breath...belly fulcrum...roll onto my back. Success! Back to front is harder. Move my arm out of the way, kick my leg, strain a bit...I'm back to my belly. It's slow going, but sufficient; five feet in the span of two minutes. I feel pretty good about this since I've never attempted to motate myself this far before.

The center of the house appears to be a tree trunk. Better lick it to be sure. Why am I like this? Ouch! No crying now. Focus. Tree bark doesn't feel good on my tongue. Better lick it again just to make sure. Stop! I'm not licking anything else!

The staircase begins just to the right of me. It spirals around the trunk. I had assumed that each step was attached to the tree and then braced by something else at the outer edge. But now I see that neither of those things are true. There is no brace on the outer edge, and the step is not attached to the tree—it *is* the tree. The steps appear to be growing out of the side of the trunk. I would say that this isn't any ordinary tree house, but a tree house does not seem ordinary to me to begin with.

"Isaac," Mother calls, "why is the baby at the bottom of the stairs?"

I didn't hear her come in the room. I don't think she caught me moving.

Father whips back into the room. "Whoah, I didn't put him there."

"Are you suggesting I did?"

"No. He must have moved himself."

"He's a little young for that," she says, giving Father a skeptical look.

"I don't know what else to tell you. I laid him down in the center of the floor to play. He spun himself around a little, but that was mostly because he was high centered on his belly. It was a little funny, actually."

"Yes, but how did he get here?"

"He must have rolled. Sometimes babies figure that out. I don't know what else to tell you. If he had a middle name maybe you could use it to scold him for moving without permission," Father suggests.

"Isaac Canter Jameson," Mother snips, "that is *not* funny."

"It's a little funny," he grins.

"Fine, let's pick a name. How about Lucias Ferrick Hall!"

"I'd prefer something a little more elegant: Lucias Ferrick Jameson!"

"Ok, neither of our names. Alfred Seniful Howland."

"Celio Garland Gerrick."

"Magnifico Munchkin Mallark."

"Now you're just making things up!"

"I'm being serious about identifying the name of our child, which happens to be a very permanent thing!" Mother scoffs. "I have no idea why you are being so blithe."

"I care very much about his name, and that's why I'm putting so much thought and effort into the ones I think of.

Obviously, you're just saying whatever comes to mind at the moment."

They go on and on with endless chatter. I really do hope they pick a name for me sometime soon. I am a child without a name who lives in a tree. No one would believe me back home. Except I won't be going home. I won't be telling them anything. The urge to cry is strong this time. Might as well give in; I could use a good cry.

"Oh no, we've upset the baby!" Mother picks me up swiftly and cradles me in her arms. "It was just silliness, sweetheart. We didn't mean anything by it." She bounces me while shushing. It feels wonderful.

"Euny, dear, I do actually like the sound of Elias Jameson Hall."

"Not Hall Jameson?"

"I know it's not tradition, but it has a better ring to it with my name first and yours second."

"Oh, but Isaac, people might talk." Mother feigns embarrassment, raising a hand to her forhead. "What do you think sweetness," she says, looking down at me, "would you like to be our little Eli?"

Yes, very much and thank you. It feels lovely to have a name. It's about time. Not that I know how much time has actually passed; it's near impossible to tell with the obnoxious amount of naps I take. And it's happening again. Why is my little body so…insistent…on…sleeping…so…mu…

***

I wake up to tense whispers—not in my room, but through the wall...anxious tones. Mother is very concerned about something and Father is reassuring her. Something about me. Did I smile again? Am I not presenting the right developmental trait at the right time? Now and then Mother pulls out her parenting book and reads about what I should be doing. Maybe there's something I missed. Sometimes she'll tell me what I'm going to be doing soon. Sometimes she'll tell Father about what to expect from a certain age range. What if there's something she never said aloud? I have no means to care for myself if they find out I'm not a...normal...baby. I've tried to match all the progress points. I use some irregularity with my actions so it doesn't seem like I've been listening. What have I done wrong? This is not good. I don't know what's wrong. I can hear her footsteps. She's coming to get me. Calm...be calm.

"You're always awake, yet never a sound. Why don't you fuss? Why are you such a perfect little munchkin?"

I really need to work on crying more often. Is that the problem? Maybe it's just that I don't cry enough. I can work on that. To do list for Eli: cry more.

"Isaac," she calls to the other room, "what if he *is* an August Child? What will we do?"

I've never heard this term before. I have no idea what month I was born in, but it can't be that simple, right? It's very easy to determine if someone is born in the month of August. They either are, or they aren't. End of discussion. And why would that cause so much stress?

"Euny, it will be fine. I'm sure he will pass his exam. After today you'll have nothing to worry about; and when you look back on this moment you'll realize it was just a little paranoia—understandable paranoia, but paranoia nonetheless. Let's get him dressed and go. Otherwise we're going to be late, and you know we can't be late for this."

My anxiety is through the canopy. I have no idea what's going on, and there is no analogue for this on Earth. Is it a doctor's visit? Maybe he means physical examination. It must be like a one-month checkup. But again, why is this stressful for them? I'm supposed to receive my official name soon. I'm not too accurate on how many days I've been around, but we must be somewhere near a month; and I'm certain one of them said my name isn't official until after a month. But what is an August Child and why are they so concerned about it?

I look around. Evidently, I was distracted with my thoughts as I am now fully dressed and we are waiting outside. I look back towards the house. It is a tree! Never mind that now, though. I need to focus. I see a vehicle approaching, but there's no road. Is this not a car? My assumption was that we had driven home from the hospital in a car a month prior; but I wasn't big on opening my eyes at the time, so I guess I don't actually know. There's no road anywhere, and the vehicle that's coming doesn't seem to need one. The giant, bean-shaped pod glides to our position. Actually, above our position. It hangs in the air for a few seconds, then slowly descends ten meters to ground level. It's an amalgamation of wood and metal—more wood up high, more metal down low. Steps drop down. It still hovers half a meter off the ground. Two steps up and we are in. Am I Cinderella? I don't think so, but this is a pretty impressive carriage. The wood is molded on the inside to form seats. At least seven people could fit comfortably in here. Mother holds me in her lap. No seatbelts. Interesting. The steps retract and we are completely enclosed. I feel us rise. A large window at the front and narrow windows running along the sides allow us to see where we are and where we are going: into the woods.

***

I don't see any other tree houses nearby. All I can see is a forest of oaks—in every direction—large, glorious, majestic oaks. The path is clear ahead, but it's not like a road. Grass grows beneath, completely undisturbed. There is no wear of any kind, but it's definitely a clearing for travel. Father touches his right temple. I've seen him do this before but never paid it any mind. This time, when he does it, we begin to move.

"Don't you think one month is too young for this?" Mother pleads. "He barely knows who we are right now, and he's so small. How can you hurt something that is so small?"

"Are you worried about the chip or the test?"

"Can't I be worried about both?"

"Look, everyone gets the chip put in and we don't remember it. It's barely more than a vaccine injection. It will sting for just a moment, and then it's over. As far as the test goes, let me set you at ease." Father turns to look me directly in the eyes, his manner more pensive, true concern showing on his face. "Eli, I'm certain that you are a tiny baby who has no idea what I'm saying, but just in case there's more going on inside, I should share a few things with you. Some children born on this planet remember their entire lives on Earth. It's a marvelous thing. They are called August Children. Today we are taking you somewhere you will be tested to see if you are an August Child. If you are, you will be taken away from us. The people that would take you are not good people and we want to keep you with us. I would explain more, but our time is limited. Even if we had more time, I have no more compelling argument than our love for you. In the last month, I have loved you with all my being. If you are such a remarkable child that you understand everything I'm saying to you, please stay with us. We will hide who you are and teach you everything we know."

He turns to Mother, the tension leaving his shoulders as the breath leaves his lungs. They share a moment of reassurance.

"I could not think of any better argument than our love," she says, "and thank you for settling my anxiety."

Father turns back to me, making eye contact. He knows already by my gaze—my intent clearly written in the resolve on my face. I have never spoken before. Sure, I've let out a few squawks and squeals; but I've never attempted any words for fear of giving myself away. I've been waiting to understand more, not wanting to terrify the people who love me most in this world. I know what a parent's love is. I have received it before, and I have given it to my own children. My life and my understanding would never be a reason to rebuff the unconditional love a parent has for their child. There is no facade here. I do not question their intention or motivation. It is pure. The choice is obvious.

"You are my family. I would like to stay with you."

CHAPTER 2
QUICKLY, LIE

Immediately, Father touches his temple. "Stop! Rest!" The pod comes to a halt, and I feel us lower towards the ground.

"Isaac, what are you doing?" The panic in Mother's voice is palpable. Her body is tense, her arms now rigid as she holds me. Words fly off her tongue. "We can't be late. It's very bad to be late to these things. We're going to be late if we stop and then you know if we're late they're going to run longer tests. They'll find him out! They'll take him away from us! We can't...we can't..." Her words trail off in tears.

"It is better for us to arrive late and prepared than on time and unprepared." He turns to me, compassion, love, wonder in his voice. "My son, my precious infant boy and fantastic little man; I promise you...everything is going to be fine."

***

We arrive at the Children's Center, though one could argue it was not designed for children. Giant oak trunks stand as pillars out front. As we walk past the gnarled wood, no wider than a grown man's outstretched arms between each tree, entangled roots cascade down to create twenty some odd steps the width of the building leading up to the main entrance. The canopy, nearly seven meters overhead, grows radiant flowers filling the area with soft, gold light. The size of this place makes me feel insignificant. The double doors to enter the building stand at least twice the height of Father. They are pinned open so you can walk directly into the great hall. The hall is ominous and large, the ceiling vaulted. This place is the first thing I have seen that does not blend in with the forest. It stands apart from everything else. The irony is clear when I see, engraved into the wooden floor, "We were made for the land and the land was made for us."

As soon as we enter the hall Father walks frantically toward the main attendant at the front desk. His breaths are short and fast; and his arms are waving about, almost in rhythm with his gait, but not quite. His hips move wildly with the deliberate steps of his feet. It makes me think of the mandatory walk of a child who was recently running. Still two meters from the desk, he starts spouting words fast enough that I'm surprised his tongue can keep up.

"I'm sorry; I'm so sorry! My alarm didn't go off at the right time this morning, or I guess I didn't set my alarm for the right time...something like that. Oh, I don't know! I just got here as fast as I possibly could. I'm so sorry. Really...I am! We're only a few minutes late, and I—"

"Sir, do you have an appointment today?" the woman at the desk says flatly.

"Uh, I did, I do! Yes, I do. Um...Hall Jameson...er...Jameson Hall. I know we were supposed to be here ten minutes ago, and again, I'm so sorry."

"It's fine sir." As the words fall out of the attendant's mouth, each and every one drops as a sigh of annoyance and disinterest. "It is important to be on time for these appointments, but ten minutes will not result in any legal charges against you unless you make any further attempt to delay or halt the identification and naming of your child."

"Oh, no, no, no, no, no! My child is special! I want to make sure he is given the full opportunities of an August Child. I mean, he's only one month old; but he's smiling already! I read in my wife's baby book yesterday that it's at least six weeks before a baby smiles! There can't be any other explanation, he *must* be of August. He just hasn't chosen to show us his true self yet!"

Mother, having caught up with Father, chimes in, "Oh yes, he's quite fantastic indeed! I'm near certain I heard him say his first word the other day; or, I guess in his case, it would just be 'a' word. He certainly knows a lot of words. Will we find out today if he'll be a singer or dancer or whatever other fantastic—and I won't complain if it happens to be lucrative—career he might have?"

"Ma'am, the proctor will evaluate your child soon and will give you all the details you need to know. I'll make a *special* note in your file stating that you have…questions…to ask. Identification, please."

"Oh, of course!"

The attendant looks just the slightest bit annoyed that my parents have all the proper documents in order. "Very well, now please take a seat at the far wall. Someone will be with you shortly."

We move quickly through the hall to the far wall. Our hurriedness is for naught. The relief I expect Mother and Father must feel does not show on their faces. Instead, the eagerness they expressed at the front desk slowly turns to disappointment. They act their part well. No less than an hour passes before we are called upon.

Finally, what looks to be a nurse comes to collect us, and we follow her down a long corridor and enter a circular study. Books line the shelves over the desk opposite the door. To the right sit two chairs. In the center of the room is a bassinet. We sit, Mother still holding me in her arms. Another twenty minutes pass before the proctor arrives and sits across from us in the chair at the desk.

"Welcome," he begins coldly. "I will be your proctor today. What we're going to do is a series of tests to evaluate the identity and name of your child. If there is no existing identity we shall file naming papers with the name you have chosen. If he is found to be of August he will get to decide the name that is to be filed." He motions for me to be placed in the bassinet.

"Well, we're certain you'll find our son to be exceptional." Mother's voice shimmers as she lays me down. "I just know he's one of the special ones."

The proctor stares blankly for a moment. He seems to be focused, but his eyes don't track with anything I can see. Fixing his attention on my parents again, he continues, "Ah yes, I can see that you believe your child to be of August. We will let the tests determine that, but know that you will have ample opportunity to share all of your findings with me. Our first test will evaluate his hearing."

The proctor places a sturdy pair of headphones over my ears as well as some electrodes on my head. His lips begin to move, but I can't hear his voice any longer. I would wager he is explaining to Mother and Father how this test works.

For the first thirty seconds, random clicks and tones play through the headphones. The electrodes measure the response of the hearing nerve. I've seen this on Earth before. After what seems like a complete test, a calm, male voice begins to speak.

"Child of August, we would like to welcome you to Merced. We know how you got here, and we have all the answers to your questions. We just need one small thing from you before we can begin our journey together: your name. At any point during this examination you need only tell us your name and we will rescue you from the people who claim to be your parents. Yes, it is true that they are connected to you biologically, but you are far more than biology and deserve a life that is greater than what they could provide. We will do our best to represent ourselves to you throughout this examination. Once you have learned enough, simply speak your name and we will welcome you with open arms. You will find a family of others like yourself; they will teach you and share everything with you. It is a marvelous heritage. Join us."

The proctor removes the headphones. He is mid sentence. "...and we like to be certain they can hear. That is why we run such a thorough test, being sure to cover a range of high and low frequencies at varying volumes."

That is overtly inaccurate. Evidently, bureaucracy doesn't change from one planet to the next: they lie when it suits them.

"Not to worry, the boy passed the test. This is good news," he says without a hint of optimism in his voice. "As you well know, the deaf are not to be trusted."

What's wrong with deaf people? That is oddly bigoted of him to say, yet my parents don't react to his words at all. No time to dwell; we're moving on.

"Our second test will be a test of desire. We will share with the child what life here could be."

The nurse walks into the room with a small device. She attaches two diodes to my forehead. The corresponding wires travel from my head back to the metallic object that sits in the palm of her left hand.

The proctor continues to explain, "This device shows your son's truest desires. For most infants, they just see images of their families, or maybe food, or a toy. For August Children, the device shows them everything they ever wanted from their past life on Earth and what they could have here on Merced."

The proctor's voice fades into the background and I am enraptured. I see an art gallery. People have come from all over the world to see this exhibition. The paintings are marvelous wonders—everything I have ever wished to create. Canvases fill walls and tell intricate stories. A piece containing only blue and red, shows the simplicity of love and how two opposing colors can join together to create something beautiful. Sketches litter another wall—unfinished ideas that hold the power to move people to tears. Every style I can think of is represented, but somehow it all fits together perfectly. And they are all mine. I am Picasso, van Gogh, Michelangelo. This is everything I have ever dreamed of and more. I am an artist. I know I'm an artist, but this is different. I get to focus on the only thing I have ever wanted. This could be my life. I can become a master of every style. I can be fulfilled and happy with one simple choice. This will provide meaning and depth to all of the countless hours I have spent on my craft. This is my greatest desire, everything I ever wanted. And all I have to do is look up at the proctor and tell him my name.

As the diodes come off the room appears dull—all the colors muted. The light shines less brightly. I want color in my life. I want to create. I want to be an artist that is revered around the world. I'm less concerned with the fame, but I yearn for the recognition that what I do holds value. I open my mouth and take a deep breath. I'm going to tell him my name. I love my parents, even in the short time I have known them, but this world is too dull. The light does not shine brightly enough. The colors are not strong enough. I am going to take this opportunity to become my truest self—what I have always known myself to be. I will have a life that I only dreamt of on Earth. I almost speak, but then I remember I promised Father I would do one thing after the test of desire. What was it? Ah, yes—think of my stomach. Wait, what? Why my stomach? My stomach is fine. Why should I consider my stomach when a world of beauty awaits me? This is no time to decide if I'm hungry or not—except that my stomach is not fine. It hurts! I haven't eaten in hours. The hunger pangs pull me back to reality just long enough. As I exhale it is not my name that escapes my mouth, but a blood curdling scream.

"This happens very often," the proctor reassures my parents in a dull, dry voice. He tries to continue with his explanation, but he can't be heard over my boisterous crying. After several attempts resulting in sighs of frustration, he resigns himself to explain in pieces during the small gaps of time when I am gasping for air. I could stop, but it's important to keep up appearances. Also, it is rather enjoyable to be on this end of things for once, no longer being the parent or grandparent trying to speak through the cacophony. "Children see—their favorite food in—in perfect detail and they can—almost taste it. When it's—oh, just give him a bottle, would you?" he shouts.

Mother pulls a bottle out of her bag, lifts me out of the bassinet and plunks it in my mouth. I am ravenous—far too hungry to think about anything else. I can barely hear the proctor in the background.

"When the image of a bottle, or whatever they are thinking of, is taken away, babies become very unhappy. We can't see what their desires are, but this is very *common.*" He is already certain that I am common. Excellent.

A few minutes pass and my bottle is drained. I open my eyes to a fresh view. The nurse and the proctor have left the room. The colors have returned to normal, or maybe my eyes have returned to normal. The second test presented my desires in such a way that they were more vivid in my mind than my eyes alone could perceive. In the moment, it was nearly impossible to resist. Now that I have had some time to settle myself I remember exactly what I want out of this life. I remain silent. As my mother stands to put me back in the bassinet I catch a glimpse of the clock on the far wall. Forty minutes have passed since the hearing test ended. It only felt like five.

"The third test is for the parents," the proctor says, re-entering the room. Seeing that I am done, he hands my parents a pair of bracelets. "Each of you put on a bracelet. They are linked to each other and thus link the two of you. I will ask you a series of questions. Isaac, if Eunice thinks you are lying, she will receive a shock. Likewise, Eunice, if Isaac feels that you are lying, he will receive a shock. It is nothing that does any permanent damage, but enough that you won't be able to hide it. Do you understand?"

With a devilish grin Mother lights up. "I have no idea what you're talking about."

"Aah!" Father nearly jumps out of his chair, not having expected to be shocked so soon. "Why would you do that?" His body language says he is mad. His eyes say he loves playing overtly childish and silly games with his wife.

"I just wanted to see what it was like for someone else before I got shocked. You were the only other person available, and I don't mind watching you feel a little bit of pain," she smirks.

"I don't believe you."

"Eeh!" I can see the shiver run down her spine. In a tone filled with arrogance and defiance, she follows, "Well it's just not nice to do that to a *lady*!"

The proctor's tone and manner betray a quiet exasperation, "I think we'll go ahead and skip the test examples. You folks seem to have a handle on how this works. We have five questions. The first, and most broad: do you have any reason to believe that your child is of August?"

"Yes of course!" Mother resounds. "The other day I'm almost certain I saw him roll from his back to his front!"

Father strains as the shock passes through his body.

"You don't believe that I saw the baby roll over? I mean, not that I saw it per se; but I laid him down on his back for his nap, and when I came back he was on his belly. I'm nearly certain. I mean, there is the possibility that I may have gotten it mixed up. Maybe I laid him on his belly and then he flipped to his back, or maybe he was on his back the whole time; but, whatever the case is, I'm *certain* he has rolled over."

Father's face grimaces this time. It doesn't look to be a pleasant experience.

"For the record, rolling over would not constitute any claim for a child being of August. While that behavior may be early for a baby at one month, it is not unheard of. Furthermore, lying about your child rolling over will not magically make your child of August. Please choose your words carefully." It looks like it's taking some genuine amount of effort to keep his eyes from rolling. Ever the consummate professional, he continues, "Moving on. Have either of you ever seen the baby track you with his eyes?"

"Yes!" Father rings out excitedly. "He's actually doing it right now!"

Mother's eyes shut as she lets out a small grunt. The proctor, leaning forward ever so slightly, stares down the barrel of his nose to take a scrutinizing look at my eyes. His head falls and his body returns to its otherwise unmoved position.

"Have you ever seen him grab anything that you thought was out of his reach?"

Mother, a bit more somber this time, "Um, no...I don't believe so."

"Have you ever heard him speak?"

"Yes," her eyes filling with a little more life, "I believe he called me 'Mama' the other day. Though he may have just been making sounds. And it may not have been anything at all. I was turned away when I heard a noise. I think that maybe I just wanted him to say 'Mama' so I imagined he had. Maybe he didn't say anything at all, and it was just my imagination." I remember this. Mother had been concentrating on something else. A sound came from outside the house. She turned and came straight to me wondering if I had made the noise. I think she may have embellished her story a bit, but not to the point that Father would think she is lying. Lying by telling the truth is a tricky business.

"Thank you for your honesty. The final question: have any of you conspired in any way to deceive anyone today about the identity and name of your child?"

"Well," Father starts, a little anxious, "we were a few minutes late today. We weren't trying to be, but we had to stop because our son spoke to us for the first time on the way here, and we had to make a plan about how to pass all the tests without any of us being found out."

Mother's whole body contracts and shakes for a half-second. It's perfect.

"Sorry Euny, I owed you one."

"Sir, we take these matters seriously." Anger crosses the proctor's face. It is the first substantial emotion he has shared the entire time we have been in the room. "Conspiring to conceal, and concealing an August Child is an offense that is punishable by death. For the well-being of these children with fully formed identities, we cannot allow families to keep them. Their lives would be endangered." His rebuke is over and his tone softens, "But it is clear to me that you are ordinary people who love your child and want him to be exceptional. You have an inappropriate sense of humor, and your desires are misguided; but that is not especially uncommon. We have one final test before we can fill out the paperwork and get you on your way." He reaches into his desk drawer and rattles around a bit before pulling out a small bottle. He doesn't even look to see that he got the right one—maybe they're all the same. Using the pipette dropper that doubles as a lid, he draws out liquid. In an odd manner, he stretches his arms out in front of him for a second. The bottle, now in my direct line of view, is clearly marked: CONTAINS CYANIDE.

We hadn't planned for this. What am I going to do? We planned for a lot of things, but dying because the proctor didn't check the bottle wasn't on the list. Do my parents see the bottle? Do they see that it's Cyanide? Neither of them are showing any discomfort at the fact that I will be meeting my end. Maybe I was the only one who got a clear enough view. I'm going to die, aren't I? Even if I tried I would have no way of stopping it. I'm far too weak. I make eye contact with Father for the briefest of moments. That's the emergency signal. He scrambles, eyes darting about the room. He doesn't know what's going on. I *am* going to die!

"This substance is a chemical test. We place three drops on the tongue of the child. If it turns blue the child may be of August and is sent away for further testing. If there is no color then the child is not of August."

While the proctor is talking Father continues to scan the room. He understands that something is wrong, but he doesn't know what. Finally, he locks on the bottle. He waits calmly until the proctor is done before asking, "What exactly is Cyanide? I've never heard of it before."

As the proctor tells some lie about how Cyanide is a special coloring additive, Father raises his hand and scratched his head. He is still wearing the bracelet. So is Mother. He isn't lying. He has never heard of Cyanide. The most logical reason my father would not know about Cyanide is because it doesn't exist on Merced. This is not a test about the color the liquid turns, nor did the proctor grab the wrong bottle. If an August Child revealed nothing to his parents, it is possible he could hide himself up to this point. It's possible he could deny the test of desire; or, like me, he may find himself hungry at the right moment. The parents would give nothing away because they know nothing. This test is designed to make an August Child speak—to make a plea for one's life. I will not. If my father doesn't know of it then it probably doesn't exist. Besides, killing babies would be bad for business, right?

Sugar water, and—surprise, surprise—it didn't turn blue.

CHAPTER 3
HOME

RE: Isaac Canter Jameson

Subject arrived ten minutes late for naming appointment. He was frantic, claiming his child was "special." Test results revealed nothing out of the ordinary for the child.

Subject inquired about Cyanide. The question was innocuous, though it was the first time anyone has asked about it during my tenure as a proctor. Subject seemed aloof and exceedingly attentive at different times. Further observation may be prudent. Please advise on how I should proceed.

~ Garrison

RE: RE: Isaac Canter Jameson

Isaac Jameson and Eunice Hall have been model citizens. Their work is typically flawless. Being aloof is a departure from the profile we have on them. It is common for new parents to exhibit more erratic behavior, and this is likely the case. We will mark this in their file as a yellow flag. I see multiple other yellow flags in their file, so you are correct that further observation is warranted. Please add them to your caseload and report back regularly.

Treat Jameson/Hall as a level 3 threat. I understand that level 3 typically requires evidence of treason, and we have nothing of the sort; but their skillset and the influence and respect they hold with their peers could pose problems if they discover they are being watched.

~ Ward

The Proctor, having seen all he needed, fills out the official naming papers, signs them along with my parents, and leaves. We wait another twenty minutes before the nurse returns to administer a simple procedure: a microscopic chip is being injected into my right temple and trace amounts of Garafin into the tips of each of my fingers.

No one speaks a word as we leave the Children's Center. Not until we have been traveling in the pod for several minutes does Father look me directly in the eyes and break the silence. "You must be exhausted. We now have a lifetime to answer all of your questions. You should sleep."

I hadn't considered that I was tired. I also don't remember shutting my eyes. I open them and find myself in my crib at home. Home is an interesting concept when I barely know anyone in the world. It's especially interesting when it was nearly taken away from me, but we prevailed;

and now I live in a tree! I believe this is what children on Earth would call "the dream."

Ready to see my parents and share a real conversation for the first time, I nearly call out to them, but stop myself short. I have no idea how long I have been asleep, nor do I know if anyone is in the house besides my parents. I don't hear anybody, but that gives no assurance; so, I cry.

Mother opens the door quickly and looks at me with a tinge of concern. I stop crying as soon as I see her. She pauses, thinks, then chuckles. "No one else is here, you clever little boy. Isaac," she calls out the door, "he's up!"

Mother holds me as we sit in the living room. Father starts us off, "We all have so very much to talk about. May I be the one to begin?" He asks *me* this. I nod my head. "Wonderful," he continues, "the first and most pressing matter is that of your name. Officially, you are Elias Jameson Hall. To keep you hidden from the Patricians we must maintain that on all documents. This does not, however, inhibit us from calling you by another name. What would you like to be called?"

My voice is thin—high—weak. I know how to form the words I need, but my muscles aren't familiar with the movements. What comes out does not represent anything I was on Earth, and that is exactly as it should be. "My given name is perfect. I was someone else on Earth. I remember all of it. It was a wonderful life, and I *will* tell you about it sometime; but I don't see any value in trying to recreate who I was. I am someone new. I have a new family. I have a new body. I should also have a new name. Thank you for giving me such a beautiful name, and thank you for allowing me the choice."

Mother and Father both have a few tears welling up in their eyes. I'm not going to tell them how hard this is for me at the moment. This is everything they wanted. They are overjoyed that I am a part of their family. In all honesty—especially considering my alternatives—so am I; and they don't need to know about the bitter that accompanies the sweet.

"Ok," Father continues with a smile while drying his eyes with his sleeve, "this is far less important, but I must know. What is Cyanide, and why did you look like you were about to die? I know it was just a blip of eye contact, but I was terrified!"

For the next three hours, Father, Mother and I discuss everything that happened at the Children's Center. The plan worked! Mother and Father had known about the test of desire and how insidiously alluring it is. They believe the diodes actually send impulses into the child's brain making it nearly impossible to resist. That's why they didn't feed me when we arrived at the center. Though I have the mental capacity of an eighty-seven-year-old, the hunger pangs of my infant body cannot be ignored.

The rest of the plan was simply lying. Mother and I congratulate Father on his masterful performance when we entered the great hall. He got the attendant to make a note on my file that my parents were "fanatics." He explains to me that the proctor had reviewed the information using his CI, which is basically an internal computer display, if I understand it correctly. Once the proctor believed we were fanatics, he was not able to see it any other way.

My parents knew they would be asked questions, but they didn't know what questions. They are incredibly attuned to each other; Father had not rehearsed anything with Mother. We both extolled her acting ability, pretending to receive a shock when Father told the truth.

"Your father is exceptionally predictable. He telegraphs everything from a kilometer away. All you have to do is pay attention. In his defense, I do find it hard to pay attention to him; but I still played my part better than he played his." She looks directly at him and scrunches up her nose. It is both silly and a direct challenge.

Such bravado inspires Father to grab me from her arms, at which point we both demand she recreate the fake shock multiple times for our own personal enjoyment.

"I don't know if I can do it again," she says, immediately followed by a fake shock. "Try telling a lie." Another shock. "Maybe I'll do it better." And yet another shock.

"In all my life, I have never loved you!"

Mother nearly falls to the floor as her head rolls back and her whole body spasms for a good five seconds. "You mustn't tell lies that are so big; they could get someone hurt," she says aghast. Everyone is laughing—the exact reprieve we need from such a stressful day.

I explain how I decided to remain silent in the face of imminent death, assuming Father's lack of knowledge meant that Cyanide didn't exist here. Mother, not one to miss an opportunity to playfully chide Father, shares, "I, too, have made life-altering decisions based on the ineptitude of your father. It hasn't always turned out so well." She raises her shoulders, sucks in a quick breath through her clenched teeth and shakes her head.

Next, Father explains how my implant works. "It sends a signal to the optic nerve creating a display that only you can see, even if you shut your eyes. The Garafin in your fingertips allows you to interact with what you see."

"So, it's kind of like a touch screen computer."

Blank stares. Neither Father nor Mother have any idea what I am talking about, but both are vastly interested.

"Earth history isn't allowed to be taught on Merced," Father explains. "It's actually a crime. The Patricians claim that *The Knowledge of the Possible* gives them just cause to withhold any and all information about Earth. Invariably,

August Children will share some things with the masses about their past lives; and everyone knows about the existence of Earth, but specific details are hazy at best."

"I will tell you everything and anything you want to know about Earth as long as you promise to tell me everything you know about Merced."

We are all in agreement. With a seemingly endless bevy of knowledge available to share and learn, we decide the best place to start is with our own lives. We each share our story.

***

"This is the story of Isaac Canter Jameson."

"Third person...really?" Mother rolls her eyes.

"It's my story and I'll tell it in whatever person I want! And if I decide in this moment that I want to tell it in first person, just know that it has nothing to do with you. Isaac can do whatever he wants."

We all snigger a little before he continues.

"I am an architect, though it's not quite like you might imagine it to be. I promise to teach you more about trees in the future; but suffice it to say, I write the code that transforms trees into homes. My code gets integrated into the living system of the trees, and they reshape and form over the course of a few weeks. I'm not working currently—out on paternity leave—but I work from home, so I won't be going anywhere any time soon.

"Growing up, I was always fascinated with transformation projects and the power they draw from the surrounding forest. I would seek out trees that were being formed into something new just so I could sit and watch the progress. I can't remember a time in life I didn't want to be an architect, so that's what I trained for in school. Children on Merced attend school until the age of sixteen, at which point they have the option to test into university. Students don't choose universities like they do on Earth, at least as far as I understand it. If accepted to university on Merced, you attend the closest institution. This is where I met your mother: the university in Sova.

"In my third year at university, I was tasked with programming a seed. Given the proper energy source, I was supposed to be able to watch this seed grow into something in a matter of minutes. The creation was not supposed to be complex or large, just something simple, like a miniature chair or a small tool. Now, I don't exactly like things that are simple; so I decided to program a miniature house. It would stand three decimeters tall and include everything a standard home would include...just smaller. This is where my problems began.

"Every time I tried to integrate my code with that of the seed, it would produce a small tree with comparatively giant tumors. One trial would have a front door, another would have a window; but none of them even remotely resembled a house. Your mother—who was not an architect but a biology student—saw my creation one day and suggested a minor change to my code. I tried it and invited her to come watch my next trial. She was very pretty—"

"*Is* very pretty," Mother corrects.

"Yes, yes—of course: was and continues to be. As I was saying, it was the least I could do to invite her to my next trial. Luckily for me, it worked! And she was awed by the beauty of my little creation. That was the beginning of the end for me.

"And then we climbed through the Sovan hills, battled mountain goats with horns the size of the crescent moon and then jumped into the ocean and swam for days, almost dying seven times over before finally…" He pauses on my behalf. Wait, what is he saying? "You're not paying any attention to me, are you?"

I shake myself out of a daze, eyes wide with the shock of the moment. "I'm so sorry. I want to hear everything, but this baby brain makes it really hard to focus sometimes. Also, I might be hungry…or sleepy…maybe both, but probably only one. There's a whole host of overwhelmingly powerful emotions I experience that I have never had to deal with before. Did you know you can be sad because you haven't had any milk in the last hour? Also, I have a serious problem with wanting to lick things. I might need therapy."

Mother and Father both laugh. Within minutes I have a bottle in my mouth and do my best to focus on the rest of Father's story.

"Three years pass, and I take your mother on a trip into the woods. After an hour of hiking we come upon a tree stump standing two meters high with enormous tumors all over. It was the ugliest thing your mother had ever seen.

"'The last piece of code this tree needs is a simple touch of your hand,' I told her."

Mother chimes in to re-enact her own lines, recalling the moment. "The last piece of code to what—explode and never be seen again?"

"It's the beauty within that matters, right?"

"I guess that is why I'm with you…the 'beauty within,' that is."

"Make all the jokes you want," Father feigns defiance, recreating the moment perfectly for me, "but I am and have always been incomplete without you."

"So what you're saying is that you botched your code again and you need me to fix it? I guess I'll just have to help you."

"Then she touched the bark of the tree," Father continues. Their interchange is done. "All the tumors turned to dust and blew away in the wind. There was almost nothing left. A stump stood before us with a single rose growing from the center. Following my direction, we each placed a hand on the bare wood of the stump and watched as the flower came into full bloom. Not actually a rose, but a perfect re-creation made of wood. Over the next few minutes we watched the petals fall one by one and return to the stump from which they came."

Father turns his gaze towards Mother. They lock eyes as he recites what he told her on that day. "When I am old and gray and have lost all of my petals, I want to know that you are by my side. I cannot imagine a life without you."

He turns back to me. "As I said that a new flower emerged. I plucked it from the wood and handed it to your mother, saying, 'This is a token of my affection for you. Please, won't you receive it and be my wife?'"

"The ten years that followed have been the greatest of my life. This is all I ever wanted—a perfect little family."

***

"I'm not fond of recalling my childhood," Mother begins her story. "Suffice it to say, my parents made my home an insufferable place to be. For this reason, I stayed in the woods as much as I possibly could. The trees kept me safe—they were my refuge, so I began to study them. I studied for two reasons: first, because I loved them, and second, as a means of escape.

"I made a perfect score on my university entrance exam. This is extremely rare since the test covers multiple competencies. Only one mastery score is needed to enter university. I had seven. Anything over two is considered perfect. So while your father only had one option in choosing what to study, my options were almost limitless."

"Hey," Father interjects, "I was very proud of being accepted into university, and I only ever wanted to be an architect!"

"Shush now, this is *my* story!" Mother continues. "I decided to study biology because it was what I loved most. Having never met your father before, I didn't know much about him; but I had seen him over a month-long period carrying the most horrific little trees. On the day I approached him—or really, took pity on him—I gave him no small suggestion. The way he was implementing his code was fundamentally wrong. Trees have a natural code, and simple things can be integrated into them when they are seeds; but your father had been trying to integrate his complex code with that of the seed. As the tree grows up the codes cannot mix. You see, he didn't understand that the code must be implemented alongside and separate that of the tree's natural code. Overwriting the tree was causing massive failures, because his code was so complex."

"So then he invited you to see it, and you were awed by his masterpiece?"

"Not exactly." Her grin spreads across her entire face. "Your father did invite me and I went with him. I thought it was silly of him to try to do something so complex at this stage. He was in a beginner course and needed to learn the fundamentals. His code worked this time, and it looked just fine; but I had created things that were more complex, and I wasn't even studying architecture! What drew me to him was that, in the lab, he had all twenty of his previous attempts lining the wall. I asked what he was doing with them. He told me he was waiting until his trials were done, and then he would find a patch in the forest to plant them. He told me that all trees, no matter how they looked, deserved to grow and become something magnificent. Our first date was planting those trees together. I was in love. We had not chosen the same field of study, but we had the same love and admiration for everything that surrounded us.

"He also forgot to tell you that when he proposed, it was the same place we had planted those trees. He had come back repeatedly and interfaced with the trees, spending hours on each one to remove his broken code. This is no small feat. As a tree grows, its code becomes more complex, and any programming that is added into the base code when it is a seed is fragmented into a thousand parts. I knew from the moment we got to that site that he had done all of it for me. I didn't tell him this at that time. He still thinks too much of himself," she winks at him, "but I knew he must have spent days turning his monstrosities into beautiful works of art. The stump that was at the center of it all has grown into one of the most beautiful trees I have ever seen. This is a large part of the reason why—to this day—I am desperately in love with your father.

"After university, I worked directly with the vegetation in the forest; and that sent me all over Merced. A couple years ago I took a job that allowed me to spend more time at home. Now I work together with your father on projects. We work for different departments, but architects and biologists always work together. Now we collaborate on everything, and we get to create the most wonderful things. In its most simple form, your father creates a design and I decide how best to implement it, considering the needs of the tree and the surrounding vegetation.

"A few years passed and then you came, Eli." She smiles. "Now you'll have to wait to find out how my story ends."

***

"Andrew James Colfeld was my name. I grew up in the information age and saw society transform before my very eyes. When I was a young child, no one really knew computers existed. Computers are like the CI, except we didn't have the technology to connect to the optical nerve, so we created physical, tactile machines."

Mother and Father both nod in understanding.

"Computers did exist, but they were enormous. One machine would fill up an entire room. Only the very wealthy could afford them. By the time I entered university, computers had become small and were required for everything. I guess it's not very impressive compared to what we have here on Merced, but it changed my world. Everything became digitized. Businesses died unless they made a major effort to be a part of the digital society. Everyone existed digitally. We even created caricatures of ourselves to show other people the impressive accomplishments of our lives. We didn't often share the sadness, which I think ended up making people sadder than they were before. It's hard to live up to the standards of everyone's 'perfect' life. I chose a different path.

"In a time when everyone was creating digitally, I decided to create with my hands; I was an artist. You won't find me in any history book. My paintings won't be in any museums. But I was truly an artist. This was my deepest self.

"At university, it didn't matter if you were skilled at anything. As long as you paid, you could take any classes you wanted. This doesn't mean I lacked skills—I was very skilled...it's just that no one cared. So I chose to follow my passion. I studied art and art history. I knew I would continue to paint, but I also wanted to have a career that would allow me to work in the field I loved so much. After graduating I became a curator at a museum. It was a wonderful decision on my part. I was constantly inspired, and I didn't have to deal with any creative editing or lies of omission that consumed the digital world. These works of art spoke of true beauty, sadness, compassion, anger and everything else you could imagine. That was the world I wanted to live in. That world was real.

"I met Angela when I was twenty-seven. She had come to a gallery where I was showcasing my work. She was sweet; we had been talking for twenty minutes before she realized I was *the* Andrew that was putting on the show. She was mortified. I had even told her the paintings were mine, but she didn't believe me. She thought I was joking. I had no need to argue with her since she would figure it out eventually. And she did. First, she apologized about seven times in a row. Then she told me she was going to make it up to me and ran outside, practically forcing a handful of strangers to come in and take a look. To her credit, each person she nabbed stayed for at least a half hour; and two of them bought something. She was a force to be reckoned with, but she was also kind to everyone she met...that included me. I fell in love with her that very night, and I never looked back. The next sixty years were a blur.

"We had three children: Adam, Violet and Stanley. I loved each of them fiercely. They gave us eight grandchildren, and in turn five great grandchildren with at least one more on the way. My life was full—it was perfect."

Tears well up in my eyes. I can't continue. I miss them all so very much. Mother holds me close and rocks me. Ten minutes pass in silence before I can continue.

"Angela—the love of my life—passed away on September 22nd at the age of eighty-nine. I nodded off a few weeks later. We were meant to be together..." tears well in my eyes again, "...at least on Earth; and I wasn't able to make it very long without her."

I can't catch my breath. My lungs are too small. My world is spinning. I miss her so much. How am I supposed to go on without her? It wasn't supposed to be this way. The black fades and color returns to the world, though I don't remember when I lost my sight to begin with.

"I'm sorry about all the crying. I can't really help myself. I am happy that I have a new family…"

"No need to explain, darling," Mother croons. "We understand completely."

Good. I don't actually want to explain. I'm not even sure I can share any more of my story than I already have. "I feel pretty tired." I'm lying. "Would you mind laying me down for a rest?"

Mother lays me down in my bassinet, gives me a single kiss on the forehead, and lets me be. I'm not actually tired. I just want to be alone in my sorrow. Mother and Father understand, but also, they don't. I can't tell them how devastating it is to wake up and begin anew; I don't think they could handle it. It's all they would ever see when they look at me—how broken I am. This will pass with time—a long time—but that doesn't need to be their problem.

CHAPTER 4
ARIELLE

RE: Jameson/Hall Flags

I will proceed with extreme caution. What are the flags on their file currently? I would like to know exactly what I'm dealing with so I am able to be sufficiently thorough.

~ Garrison

RE: RE: Jameson/Hall Flags

Yellow Flag - Eunice Saric Hall
As a child Eunice learned sign language from a neighbor girl who was born deaf. People who befriend SOs when they are young often show sympathetic tendencies towards SOs when they are older. The indoctrination these children experience from SOs can be hard to overcome.

Yellow Flag – Isaac Canter Jameson
Isaac has limited ability to shift the wind. To our knowledge he does not possess enough skill to produce anything more than a slight breeze. He seems to enjoy this small connection with the past. We do not look down on anyone who

practices such small feats, but we do keep records of their progress when we can. A little wind being shifted solidifies our position and helps people remember everything laid out by the Triumvirate. A true wind walker could disrupt everything.

Yellow Flag – Jameson/Hall

Jameson and Hall visited the SOs in Evanwood on official business. We flagged this because they were the only people to volunteer, though they only offered after the request had been put out for more than three weeks.

Yellow Flag – Jameson/Hall

We have a third hand account of Jameson and Hall being sympathetic towards "true peace." They either used the phrase directly or did not object to hearing someone else use the phrase. This account was obtained through standard interrogation techniques of one of our "informants." It may be less than reliable, but nothing bad ever comes of keeping immaculate records.

~ Ward

I wake the next day to find that Mother is traveling to the local market and Father has already decided on a new game for us to play. It's a simple game called "Questions!" He is adamant that the title of the game should include an exclamation point since he is so very excited about it.

"The premise of the game is simple," he tells me. "Each of us have innumerable questions for the other, so we trade off answering questions the other asks; and no one is allowed to ask a question two times in a row."

This is a game I can really get into. Mother and Father have promised to start my education soon, beginning with history lessons; but I am bursting at the seams with questions.

"The best games have rules," he continues, "governing who should even take the first turn. I think, in this game, the youngest player should have the opportunity to ask the first question. So, my son, would you like to begin?"

"I *would* like to, but I'm a little worried about your ability to follow the rules." I love this type of game and we have no shortage of time—might as well make an event of this. "First, you asked me a question. If you believe that I am the youngest player in the room, which seems to be your disposition, then you should have told me to start the game—per the rules—and refrained from asking a question. Second, I am not the youngest player in the room. Nowhere in the rules does it state that 'youngest' refers to biological age. I am, in fact, eighty-seven years old, you know. You should ask the first question."

Father's face is a bright and shining star. He can barely contain himself. Using the most formal voice and manner he has, he speaks contritely. "My apologies for committing such an atrocious act in our first official game ever played together. It was not my intention to devalue the merits of our game with suppositions that were incorrect. I would like to express my deepest regrets. Now, I understand that I should begin." He pauses—the devil in his eyes tells me exactly what is coming next. "Would you like it to be your turn now?"

This is the best kind of game! "How do the windows in the house work?"

"It's amazing, isn't it?"

"That's a question."

"Colloquial turn of phrase that aligns myself in mutual admiration of the topic at hand."

"Rebuttal approved, proceed."

"We can program the trees to do nearly anything. In this instance, the wood becomes very thin and the pigment is removed from the grain. If you would like, I can take you close to it so you can see." He's careful not to *ask* if I want to see.

"Yes please!"

It's marvelous. I can see how it's a part of the surrounding wood, and not placed into it as one might assume. I can even feel the grain as I brush my hand across it. I could stare at it for hours.

"Ok, my turn," Father blurts out. "How did you keep your composure when you were born? I think I would have lost my mind upon waking up in a new world with a new body."

"Simple, that wasn't the first time I woke up."

Father's eyes become wide with shock as he realizes the implications. He's speechless.

"I had plenty of 'freak-outs' in utero. I would get a wave of panic and anxiety; I'd move a little bit, and then I'd be really tired and fall asleep. Sleep fixes a lot of things. By the time I woke up in the actual world, I was pretty settled into the idea of my new life. That's not to say that things didn't still concern me. I was just more emotionally prepared to deal with it. Don't get me wrong, though; I'm still in a bit of an existential crisis. Questions fly through my head all day long like: How did I get here? What is the nature of existence? How do souls exist? Is there an afterlife? Am I *in* the afterlife? Is there a dimensional—or possibly non-dimensional—space where it is possible to travel at a speed that is faster than light? Or did I travel slower than the speed of light and now Earth is a million years older? What happens after I die on this world? Do I go somewhere else? Is this the end?"

I look up. Father is grinning ear to ear at my flood of questions. He finds it more funny than alarming. I don't know if I'm disappointed or happy—maybe both. "I was only stating those questions, not asking them."

"I know," he says with a single laugh.

Back to the game. "Did you know it's very, very cold for that first little bit in a new world?"

"Should we tell your mother that your first memory on Merced is about how cold it was and not her loving embrace?"

"Not all truths must be told." We both laugh. "Do we know where Earth is?"

"We have a general idea. Only August Children would know what to look for to find Earth, but I don't know if there have ever been any that were astronomers. Even if one of them knew what to look for, the Patricians aren't interested in people learning much about Earth. We have been told that we do exist in the same universe, but Earth is at least seven billion light years away. If we knew exactly where it was, there still wouldn't be any means of communication or contact. I'm sorry, were you hoping to see your family again?"

"I miss them, yes; but our parting was sweet, not sorrow. Mostly, it was curiosity." A half-truth—my heart aches, but I would rather be the only one with an aching heart. My turn again. "You said the trees can be programmed to do *almost* anything. What did you mean?"

"Excellent question. The trees actually have a will of their own. They are slow moving and can be forced into position, but they will not remain in that position very long if they do not want to. For example, if you programmed a tree to move its roots away from its water source, it would comply initially. After a few days, though, the roots would return to the water. You may have noticed that the Children's Center was a little out of place compared to everything around it. They have half a dozen architects updating the code on a daily basis so the structure doesn't revert to a more natural form. Your mother and I believe that you should never program a tree against its will. Homes are an interesting feature here; the trees respond really well to having people live inside. It ends up being mutually beneficial. We get a place to live and they get fed."

I stare at Father in silence, willing him to expound. I desperately want to know what he means, but can't ask a question—it isn't my turn.

"Did you want to ask me something about that?" We both smile.

"How do the trees get fed?"

"Oh, of course, I'm sorry. Some things are so normal to me that I don't even think to explain. Everything we have on Merced comes from the land, and everything returns to the land. I've heard stories of Earth and giant mounds of waste. We don't have that problem here." Father walks me into the kitchen to show me the waste chute. "Everything we no longer need gets discarded here. This chute goes down to the root system of the tree, which works to help any material decompose. Then it gets pushed out into the soil, effectively fertilizing this tree and several others around it. *We were made for the land and the land was made for us.* We live in harmony together."

"That's one of the most wonderful things I've ever heard of. I love it so much. Thank you for sharing. Waste was a really big problem on Earth. It's wonderful that it's just a part of the natural order here. Okay, your turn."

"Do you remember the void, traveling from Earth to Merced?"

It's constantly on my mind. "Yes, though it was a different kind of consciousness. I wasn't aware of myself, but I was aware of what was around me. There was a current that moved the souls—or whatever it was that I saw—from Earth to Merced, each one a wisp of color unique to itself. It was a river filled with rainbows. I was above the current. I watched as they all passed me by. When I turned to observe my surroundings, there was nothing—black—darkness. Nothingness might be a better way to put it. It was devoid of anything. Except, I do remember, off in the distance there was a faded blue glow, like the color of the sky when the sun has almost broken the horizon. It held the dark of night and light of day in one color as if to say our day had both begun and ended, or maybe the other way around. I don't know what it was but it was beautiful and meaningful to me at the time. After a few minutes—or what may have actually been hours or days—I returned to the current. I was swept into a warm light. It became brighter and the current moved faster. Faster and brighter, faster and brighter. The light finally became blinding. Then there was darkness. My next memory was waking in Mother's womb. And yes, I was confused and terrified. Fortunately, the stress of the situation was so intense that I fell asleep almost immediately. I'm only human and I can only handle so much. Wait, am I human?"

"Ha! We do classify ourselves as human, though I haven't the slightest clue if we actually share the same DNA as our namesakes on Earth. So as far as I know, yes, you are human. What's the biggest difference you have seen between Earth and Merced?"

"The trees—by far, the trees. We have trees on Earth, and even oak trees like the ones here, but not in the same manner. There's no way to program trees to do anything, or at least no one knows how. As people on earth create cities, they cut down trees to use as materials. Our cities are vast, but they destroy the vegetation that existed previously. They have beauty in their own way, but it was definitely at the expense of the Earth. It's amazing to see how everything interacts harmoniously with the trees here. I am constantly perplexed." Before I can finish my thought, my jaws involuntarily stretch open as wide as they possibly can. The yawn is epic. And now I have no idea what I was going to say. "Evidently, I'm getting a little tired, but I have one more question for you if you don't mind: how long are the days here? I feel like I take way too many naps, but maybe that's just me getting used to being a baby."

"Thirty-six hours. Is that not how long they are on Earth?"

"No. Only twenty-four, and that's your last question!"

"Fair enough," Father chuckles. "We have about twenty-four hours of daylight. We haven't been outside much, so you may not have noticed. There are two stars in our sky, three moons and another planet. Earth just orbits one star, right?"

"I'm sorry, but the rules of the game have made it very clear," I yawn, "that you are not allowed to ask," yawn again, this time longer, "two questions—" I am interrupted by the mother of all yawns. It feels amazing and I'm so very sleepy. I can't stop, so I finally just speak through it with my mouth open wide, "in a row." My eyelids are sandbags. The last thing I see is Father's loving face as he lays me down in my room.

***

When I awake, I can hear that Mother is home. Father is still here—someone else too. I haven't heard another voice yet, but there's an extra set of feet—not loud, but a different gait than both Mother and Father. I fuss. Father comes into the room. He fills me in while picking me up.

"We have a new…friend at the house today. She knows nothing more than the fact that you are a baby."

I nod my head with a long blink of my eyes. He knows I understand.

Once in the living room I see a small girl, maybe four years old. Her dark curls hang just above her shoulders. Her lips are slightly pursed and her eyes are wholly focused on Mother. She is wearing boots that are comically large, extending up beyond her knees. I have to be careful not to laugh; the boots don't match her demeanor at all. She is resolute, persistent, steadfast. She and Mother are engrossed in conversation, at least as far as I can tell. She's deaf. I never learned sign language; I guess I will soon. As I watch, I understand small pieces. She's very emotive as she communicates and some signs are very obvious. She wants to learn. I've seen that one before. Her body language suggests she's desperate to learn. She seems very intelligent for such a small girl, and her dexterity is on par with someone at least twice her age. Where are her parents?

Mother almost looks angry, but not at the girl. She turns her head towards Father. "Did you catch all that?"

"Mostly. I missed a little while I was getting Eli, but I still followed."

"What do you think?"

"I don't know." Father frowns pensively. "I think we need to talk about it as a family, but we have to do something. I know we heard things might be bad for her, but I didn't think it would be this bad...they were right to be worried."

"I agree. Even if it was just once a week. We could say she's helping us watch Eli when we go back to work."

"Do you think she can keep it a secret?"

"She was discerning enough to choose me after a very short interaction. She didn't say anything that could have incriminated her at the time even though I'm fairly sure I was the only one in the crowd that could sign. She waited until inside our home to tell us what she needs."

I'm not entirely sure what's going on; but the girl is obviously in need, and my parents aren't ones to overlook the needs of others. I am mostly intrigued—only a little concerned. The girl's face is filled with anticipation as she watches my parents talk. You can tell that she wants to tap her foot as if to say, "Are you done yet?" but she refrains. She has no idea what they are saying. I have never seen such a young child be so much in control of herself amidst such distraught emotions. I guess I'm the exception to that, but that's beside the point.

"Let's have her return at the beginning of the week," Father says. "I think we could tentatively plan on once a week. We'll talk more, but she wants to learn so badly. It should be a crime to keep her from being educated; instead, she breaks the law by even trying." He shakes his head.

Father's hands are occupied with me, so Mother relays the information to the girl. She is elated—literally jumping up and down with excitement. She thanks Mother and Father probably ten times and even thanks me a couple times. It is delightful. Then she's out the door and gone.

I wait patiently as Mother shuts the front door and comes back to speak with Father and me.

"I'm sorry to spring that on both of you. I had only intended to observe her from a distance, but she was just such a sweet little girl that needed help. One of the grocers at the market wouldn't sell her anything. I gave him a quick rebuke, emphasizing that she is just a little girl. Afterword, I asked her a few questions; and she asked to come to my home to speak with me. She was very insistent. I couldn't say no."

"Euny, it's fine. We just have some explaining to do."

Mother shuts her eyes and takes in a slow breath. She opens them and looks at me. "Eli, we are going to give you a real history lesson soon, I promise; but today you need to learn about the Silent Order. You are keenly aware of August Children and their abilities. The Silent Order are...they...well...most people on Merced believe the Silent Order were awful people on Earth and their deafness in this life is some kind of cosmic punishment."

"So the proctor *is* bigoted! I had wondered why he said the deaf were not to be trusted."

Father lets out a loud laugh. "Don't share that sentiment with anyone, it could get you in trouble. But yes, you are absolutely correct, though no one here is willing to be quite so succinct about it."

Mother continues, "It's illegal for someone of the Order to be educated, and it's also illegal for them to be anywhere near an August Child. The Patricians tell us that envy consumes the Order, so much so that they would kill those of August.

"Arielle is the name of the girl and she is a child of the Silent Order. Your father and I do not share the opinion of the Patricians. We believe it is grossly inappropriate to treat a group of people with such disregard, but we also want you to be able to make an informed decision. I apologize for my bias, but this is an issue that is close to my heart."

I'm still deciding what I think. It's a lot of information to take in all at once. I'm sure I'll end up agreeing with Mother and Father, but processing all of these thoughts first is important to me. "She seems very intelligent—far more intelligent than any child on Earth at her age. Am I wrong? I don't know sign language, so I couldn't actually tell what she was saying."

"You're not wrong," Father says. "That was the most coherent conversation with a four year old I have ever witnessed. Do note that you are not four years old yet."

"Are all children on Merced this smart?"

"No." Mother closes her eyes and shakes her head. "From what I have seen, they are not. Those in the Silent Order, however, do seem to learn at a marginally faster rate, at least when given the opportunity. Arielle appears to be unique. Her parents decided to keep her, despite the social stigma, but won't allow her to be educated. But, as you well know, the law does not generally stop us from doing what we believe to be right. Most children who are born deaf are sent to the Order in Evanwood. They have a village there where they care for each other. They provide some informal education, but it's not nearly as robust as what another child would receive going to school. Arielle is in an unfortunately unique position: if she is going to learn at all, it will be from us."

"Then I don't think we have a choice in the matter. She obviously chose us. Now we must choose her. I may be small and vulnerable, but I cannot allow a young girl who is hungry for knowledge to be denied what should be her right."

"Eli," Father warns, "please understand that this would be very dangerous."

"I have lived a full life. I'm glad to have this one, but I don't want to have it at the expense of others. If the two of you think we can reasonably accomplish this, then I'm all in. Have you met her parents?"

"No, but they obviously know how smart she is. They sent her to the market alone, figuring she could handle herself in a crowd at four years old! And even still, they won't educate her!" Mother's face is red. "I'm sorry, I'm getting off track. When I spoke with the grocer I signed to Arielle to explain what was going on. She told me that no one has ever chosen to speak with her before, aside from her parents. She would talk with others from the Order if she could, but her parents don't let her spend time with them. They don't want to have any association with The Order—Arielle being their only exception. I asked if her parents were educating her. She said no and immediately asked to visit our home. She could tell I was sympathetic. You both saw her impassioned plea to learn. And she was smart enough not to ask in public as she knows it's illegal." She pauses. "I'm rambling now, aren't I? I've said all of this already. I'm sorry, it just upsets me so much."

"Euny, it's fine. I think we need to start a secret school! Sending Eli to school would be a complete waste. I mean, maybe they could help him learn to quit licking things, but that's about it."

"I'm so sorry! I can't stop!"

"My arm though, really?" Father says, looking disdainfully at the soggy patch of hair on his forearm.

I look at both Mother and Father with pleading eyes. "I just...I just wanted to know what it felt like."

"And..." Father implores.

"It's terrible; worse than I imagined! Can we get back to the secret school thing now? And pay less attention to how often I lick things?"

"Certainly," Father smiles. "If we already have one student, it won't take much additional effort to have a second."

We agree to proceed cautiously with Arielle. There is danger involved, but for Mother and Father there is danger with me in the house to begin with; so nothing is new. They seem confident that we can be successful, and I have no reason not to trust their judgement in the matter.

We will need to let Arielle in on my secret, but it's clear to all of us that she will agree to do anything she has to in order to learn. Hopefully, keeping my secret won't be any more difficult for her than keeping her own.

Mother and Father make preparations over the next few days. They need to start working again, but not because their leave is over—they have a lot more time left. The cover for Arielle is that they need help. She will be tasked with taking care of me and doing some other chores around the house. It wouldn't be a realistic cover unless they return to work. I make my own preparations by learning sign language. Mother and Father show me a few signs as they go about their business. I lay in the living room practicing over and over and over. It isn't very hard to remember what the signs are, but doing them myself is another feat altogether. My limbs barely do what I want them to as it is. Sign requires a bit more precision and muscle memory. I need to train my arms and hands how to work properly. I am determined to be able to communicate with this vibrant little girl as we learn together.

CHAPTER 5
SCHOOL

RE: Jameson/Hall Development

It has come to my attention that James Howell Landen and Savana Shendal Rhome have filed a form for their daughter, Arielle Linivette SO, to be a maidservant to a family with a new child. The family is not specifically named, but after some digging I have discovered them to be none other than Jameson/Hall. While this is not specifically incriminating, it does add to the growing body of evidence we have against the family. I would request this be placed in their file as an additional yellow flag. You were right to suggest this be treated as a level 3 threat. Something must be going on here and I will find out what it is.

~ Garrison

RE: RE: Jameson/Hall Development

It has been added to their file. Thank you for your diligence. This could be nothing; simply a family taking advantage of a unique opportunity. Since Eunice already knows how to sign she could make very effective use of the SO girl. I do agree with you, however, that it is suspicious. I want to make an example of this family if they are, in fact, doing anything untoward. Typically, we would stamp out a family with so many yellow flags, but without real evidence against them, this family in particular could be viewed martyrs as opposed to traitors, and we cannot have that. Keep watching them. They will make a mistake eventually and we will be waiting and ready.

~ Ward

The first day of school has arrived; the house fraught with anticipation. I lay in my bassinet in the living room as Mother and Father dart every which way. Dishes are piled up in the sink; clothes are scattered about the living room floor. Mother isn't wearing the same color socks. Father's hair is either an incredible work of art or the biggest mess of a mop I have ever seen. A knock comes from the front door. Everyone holds their breath for a fleeting second before Father rushes to pick me up and Mother goes to the door. I start to fuss as she opens it. Arielle stands at attention with her parents. Mother welcomes them all in.

"Arielle tells us you want her to help clean things?" her father says skeptically.

"As you can see, we recently had a baby." Mother points to Father who is doing his best bounce in an attempt to get me to stop crying. "And we are both returning to work today. We work from home, which means little Eli can be at home with us; but things are already falling apart a bit."

She sweeps her arm out, directing their attention to the mess everywhere. "After seeing how competent Arielle was at the market, I realized I just *must* have her come help us in our home. She's not in school, right?"

They will never know the contempt Mother holds for them. She is brilliant at weaving a lie.

"No, obviously not." Arielle's mother is terse. She wants to make certain everyone understands they are following the laws.

"Exactly," Mother assures, "and I was thinking that helping us around the house would save you from putting her in some sort of day care. It would help us immensely, and it might give her a skill that would be useful later in life. We all know she won't be good for anything else." Mother will apologize to Arielle later even though she can't hear what's being said.

"How often do you want her?" Her father—while still skeptical—is picking up interest.

"We'll see how today goes to be sure; but we were thinking every weekday, since we are working, and possibly some weekends too, depending on how much of a mess everything is and how quickly she works." Mother lowers her eyes to look down at Arielle, almost speaking directly to her. "We think it's important she understand a job is not complete at a specific day or time, but when every part of it has been finished." Her bigoted, conniving alter-ego is laying the groundwork for Arielle to be with us every day of the week.

"She will have to walk," Arielle's mother says abruptly. Her voice is also a little shaky, like she's expecting resistance. "We don't have the time to bring her here every day. It's not a short trip. But maybe the walk will be good for her." She must lie to herself every day about the life her daughter is living. There's love there, but it's misguided at best.

All the adults shake hands; a deal has been struck. Arielle's parents—who are leery, but very pleased with the arrangement—say a quick "goodbye" and leave. I doubt they'll ever visit again.

As soon as the door is shut, Mother's leg is wet. Arielle is latched on; tears streaming down her face creating a nice round circle in the fabric of Mother's pants. With some force, Mother pries her away, kneels down and gives her a true hug.

My sole focus for the last three days has been to learn as much sign as I possibly can. I am able to catch the gist of a conversation and fill in the blanks by reading body language. Mother is telling Arielle everything that was discussed, saying that she is welcome here anytime. Something else is signed and she looks at me...my turn.

My hands are not my own, unaccepting of any position I move them to. I pull against the erratic force that sways them about. This will be easier someday; but for now, I must make do.

"Hello, my name is Eli and I am of August."

Arielle lets out an audible gasp. She's frozen. Then her face lights up as she frantically signs, "He's not a normal baby? He can talk? He understands? Can he be my friend? I've never had a friend before."

"I have no other friends. You are my first, only, and best." At least that's what I hope I said. The wrinkles in her forehead make me think I haven't said anything of the sort. I'll try again. "Yes. Please. Always."

***

After sharing a meal together, we gather in the living room to begin our studies. I am beside myself with excitement. Father speaks for me and signs for Arielle, though not always at the same time. "Our first step is dealing with your Cortex Computational Imaging Implant."

We both give him a blank stare.

"It's your internal display, or 'C-I.' You were both injected with a chip a month after you were born. I'm going to show you how to use it."

I had forgotten about the chip; so much had happened since visiting the Children's Center. Father instructs us to touch our right temples. Immediately, I see a display appear before me. It's raw data that reminds me of an HTML webpage that has lost connection with its style sheet. I read everything carefully. It's all my biometric information: pulse, blood pressure—even height and weight. It isn't particularly aesthetically pleasing, but it's useful, nonetheless.

"Arielle, I'm going to get Eli started on something and then will help get you set up with a language program in a minute so you can start learning how to read."

"I can read." Her eyes shift back and forth between us as if she's not sure if she'll be believed.

"Very well, then," Father says with a sly grin, "let's begin. You should see all your vital signs: heart rate, blood pressure, etc. You might notice that it's not laid out very well. One of the first tasks every student learns is to program their display. The same is true for you. You're able to interact with your display because of the Garafin that has been injected into your fingertips. For today, suffice it to say, Garafin is an element that is responsible for many of the wonderful things that have been accomplished on Merced. But enough about that; today is for programming.

"The chip knows your exact age, weight and height. It can even list out the length of your arms and your legs. It should come as no surprise that everything you need to interact with is comfortably within your reach. You should see a virtual keyboard below your display. Eli, in your case, the keyboard will be...simplified...to accommodate your level of dexterity."

As I reach out and touch the virtual keys the garafin in my fingertips helps me feel a small amount of resistance. Once my hands are steadier I won't have to look at the keyboard when typing. For now, I'll make do. With nearly all of my physical limitations accounted for, I can begin. Learning will commence quickly!

We are only a few minutes in, working on our displays; but Arielle is upset. She's set on figuring things out for herself, but I can see the frustration building rapidly. Another minute passes and she finally gives up, deciding it is beyond her abilities. "I can't change anything!" she signs forcefully.

"Oh dear," Father gasps, "I had forgotten. Let me show you how to share your screen with me." He walks Arielle through the process and continues to explain. "The Silent Order are only allowed rudimentary access to their CI. It will track your vitals and allows simple communication when synced with a console, but that's it. The reason they allow the Order to even have the chip is for identification purposes. Fortunately for us, the Patricians are too lazy to create a chip with less facility; they just limit your abilities by way of the programming. And luckily for you, I know exactly what to change in the program to give you full access. Just seventeen lines of code and I'll...be...done!"

I am certain Father broke the law by giving Arielle full access to her CI, but he doesn't seem concerned in the least. I guess we're all lawbreakers in this house. "What happens when they scan her now? Won't they know that someone tampered with the program?

"Excellent question. It's good to consider the risks of all our actions. Some choices, like keeping a child from the

Patricians," Father looks directly at me, "or educating a young girl," he turns to Arielle, "are worth the risk. Others are not. In the case of Arielle's CI, there's really no real risk. Yes, it is illegal, but no one can see your display or access your programming unless you let them. Without Arielle's explicit consent and cooperation, I would not have been able to help her. When she is scanned it will only show her identification—same as always."

Father proceeds to show us some basic programming techniques by sharing his display with us, which pops up as a secondary screen in my vision. Everyone on Earth learns to program, so while I haven't used this language before—if they even call it that here—the concepts are the same. After an hour on my own, I have something passable. The data on my display is organized. It no longer lacks structure. It's utilitarian, but that will do for now, considering how much effort goes into controlling my wayward arms. Both Arielle and I share our displays. Hers is even better than mine. This is going to be fun.

***

Mother paces the room as Ari and I race to complete our programming. "Remember," she cautions, "the goal is to create a sequence that is not just functional, but also elegant. You must work alongside the code of the seed and not overwrite it."

We understand completely. The code must be pristine and we must take care not to disrupt the natural order of the tree. We also understand that whoever finishes first is going to win, and we are in a dead heat. Ari has proved to be my equal, or counterpart, at nearly everything we do. Her creations look different than mine, but are equally complex. In truth, because of the background knowledge I have, I could likely surpass her in programming. She spends more time learning it than I do, but Mother and Father have tasked me with learning more topics than Ari. She learns everything that is important. I learn—well—everything.

"Done!" Ari's voice rings out. She has a nasal tone when she speaks, and not every word comes out perfectly; but it's surprisingly clear. "I get to run mine first," she sneers at me. She loves every moment of this just as much as I do.

I'm finished with my code as well. We take our seeds to the accelerated growth chamber. Mother and Father added this to the home once we reached college level coursework. They never program any more into the house than what we need, and even then, only once we need it. Whenever something like this comes up they always repeat, "We were made for the land, and the land was made for us." Ari and I have heard this so often now that we roll our eyes nearly every time it's said. This only provokes Mother and Father to follow up in an obligatory fashion, "We know you memorized it after the very first time we said it. The repetition, then, shows our commitment to this value. The trees we live among are unique; they must be treated with care. And we want to instill this value in you." Yeah, we get it. Let's move on already.

The growth chamber connects to four other trees outside of our home and harnesses their power. That power is used to accelerate the growth of seeds so we can see our simple code grow quickly. The chamber could be connected to fewer trees, but we don't want to stunt the growth of a single tree by pulling too much power away from it. For our little experiments, four is plenty. This is similar to how homes are built, though they require much more power and take significantly longer to fully form.

Ari's seed begins to grow inside the chamber. It's an oak tree, but instead of leaves there are flowers. Dahlia blooms cover the branches. In between, pushing through the petals on the outer ring, wildflowers sprout up. It's beautiful.

Mother reviews the code and points out a few things Ari could do to improve. "Elegance over utility." She always says this loud enough for Father to hear, even if he's in another room. A little jab.

"That's why I married you," Father hollers back, "you may not be good for much, but you sure are pretty!"

In the five years I have lived with my parents, they have never once said something cruel to each other. It makes me think of the life I had with my Angela. Sometimes I miss her so much I feel like I'm going to explode—then it passes.

Being a child is different than I thought it would be. I had assumed the emotional maturity I obtained on Earth would limit how childlike I feel, but that is not the case. It's true that I play with a different set of toys than most children, but my physiology is the same. When I look in the mirror I see a young boy with a ruddy face and dark hair that flies in the face of order. It's hard to get used to how I look, since it changes so constantly. It's also hard to get used to how I feel. At any given moment I can experience sweeping tides of joy or sadness or anger or contentment. Every normal emotion and desire that children feel, I feel too. My emotional maturity is what allows me to navigate how I respond to those emotions. I don't lay on the floor screaming, but I still *feel* like laying on the floor screaming at times. I am fiercely competitive. The blood that pumps through my five-year-old body demands that I win at everything I do. I'm sure I would find less joy in this, except that Ari is determined to beat me at everything. She doesn't care that I'm younger than her; she knows my background gives me distinct advantages.

I place my seeded pot in the growth chamber. On top of it I have placed a single twig with a slight bit of metal attached to it. Father helped me with that part. "With the right code," he explained, "you can get a tree to find unrefined metal in the ground. It can pull it up and meld it into some wood." It can take about a month, but I've been planning on doing this for quite some time; and Father was very willing to help in my endeavors, despite the fact that I refused to explain my end goal. This will be his first peek into my intentions; certainly, Mother will share my results with him. He'll find out more tomorrow.

"What is that on top?" Mother is curious.

"It's part of my project. You'll see in a moment." The guidelines for this project were loose. We were to create something using all the programming tools we had learned. Both Ari and I love learning and trying things out so much that we are rarely given specific tasks to complete any more. We enjoy telling Mother she's being lazy by making us come up with the content on our own. Knowing how much we love to create, she always threatens to assign us something specific. We typically follow the threat with silence, furiously working on the assigned project.

As the acceleration chamber begins to run, four sprouts come out of the dirt simultaneously. They create a square that surrounds the little twig. As they grow up and branches sprout, the twig in the center begins to rise. I have been studying the code used to allow the pods to fly through the forest. The trees are their own power source and can create an electromagnetic field by using the Garafin that is in their limbs. Adding metal to the pods fixes their charge so they can float through the air on this invisible throughway.

Mother is impressed with my work. "What is this?" A line of code has caught her attention from the file I gave her, "And how did you…?" she trails off.

"I was curious what would happen if I integrated a question into the base code of the tree. I didn't want to overwrite the tree's code, but wanted to try and interact with it."

"What was your question?"

"Father said that trees have a will of their own, so I decided to ask the seed if it would help me create something. I told it what I was trying to build. I thought that sharing my intention might improve the overall relationship between my code and the tree."

"You placed your question in the base code, though...and it hasn't ruined your project. I don't understand quite how you did it, but the tree seems to have paired better with your code because of it. It's beautiful, Eli. Excellent work."

Mother finds several errors in my code. I work to fix them quickly and save the program. We are already over time. Ari has to get home, but we stand together waiting, even though she'll be late.

"Oh, both of your creations were great," Mother says, brushing us off. "If I must say, it's a tie."

"But we want to know who won!" we announce in unison.

"But it is a tie. There's nothing I can do about that."

"Eunice," Ari says as politely as possible, "I really need to go home, but I can't until we know who won."

"If I have to choose a winner, it's...Isaac!"

"I love winning!" we hear from the other room.

We both glare at Mother.

"Fine. Eli won today. Since I have never seen someone integrate anything into the base code–"

"…successfully," Father hollers.

"Since I have never seen someone *successfully* integrate anything into the base code—and that's not something you should be proud of dear—Eli is the winner today."

I stick my tongue out at Ari to rub it in. She grants me the same courtesy. Then we run. She'll be late if we don't hurry.

For the last year I have met Ari every morning at the halfway point between our homes. We created a path through the woods to minimize the distance we have to walk. In the evening, I go with her halfway and then return. We aren't very active as we study, so being outside and walking is good for us. Despite being deep in the woods, we are only allowed to sign outside of the house. Ari learning to vocalize isn't strictly illegal, but my parents are sure it would be if it was known that a member of the Silent Order could learn how.

I've met many people, but Ari is my only friend. No one else knows that I am of August. No one else has been my companion for the last five years. Making friends my biological age would be a bit of a chore; we wouldn't exactly have common interests. Ari is a bit older than I am, but also driven in a way I've never seen the likes of for someone her age.

Today, like every other day, we part ways at the halfway point; but instead of returning home, I wait until Ari is out of sight. Mother and Father know where I am, but I refused to tell them exactly what I was up to. I continue on the path towards her house. Once I am a single kilometer away, I interface with the closest oak to me and implement the code from the seed trial this morning. After several hours, I have made my way home and programmed every tree along the path.

***

I wake up early—excitement brimming through my entire body—and run out the door so I can meet Ari near her house. She's surprised to see me, but also happy. She is far more expressive than I could ever be; her left brow stands like a mountain disrupting the even plane of her forehead. She's asking what I'm doing.

"Let me show you." I pull two helmets, vests, and chaps from behind a tree, each made of wood with small pits of metal interrupting the grain at various points. "Get dressed!" We each put on our set. This was months in the making under the purposefully unwitting supervision of Father. Once dressed in my new gear, I draw an invisible line in the ground with my foot; I walk back towards Ari's house about four meters, then sprint towards my line as fast as I can. When I reach it I jump head first, arms stretched out in front of me...and I fly.

My speed and direction are actually controlled using my display. The running was just for show. Ari—having seen my project yesterday—knows this implicitly and catches up to me without any running involved. It would be dangerous to try and travel this way on the main throughways. We can't risk being seen doing anything abnormal, or things that are above our typical age levels; but we've never seen anyone on our path through the forest, and it is somewhat shrouded by the trees. To maximize our cover, I programmed our flying path to be only a meter off the ground.

What normally takes two hours to walk takes us twenty minutes to fly. Without the morning walk, my parents will certainly find other ways to get us some exercise; but that doesn't bother us one bit. Reducing travel time means that we get to spend more time together, and nothing is more important than the time we spend together. We dream and imagine with each other; I feel lost when she's not around.

Mother and Father have just gotten up; they haven't even begun to think of breakfast as we enter the house. They pause and look at us in silence. We can't help but laugh a little.

"And how are we receiving you so early this morning?" Father says with a bemused smile.

"I made a new toy."

Both Ari and I grin like...like the little children we are. Consequences are generally mitigated when the two of us are in cahoots.

"You remember how I told you yesterday that I ask the trees a question and tell them my intention?"

Mother nods.

"Well, I didn't tell you exactly what my intention was. My real intention was to create a system of travel that would reduce the time it takes Ari to get here." At this point we pull out the suits we have been hiding behind our backs. We weren't hiding them well, but it makes for a more dramatic reveal. Both Mother and Father get up to examine the suits, and we are outside within minutes so we can show off how they work. While they both understand the value of reducing Ari's travel time, they are also concerned about our safety. Whatever plans we had for school today are scrapped. Instead, the four of us work together to modify the program I had created. Mother sets it up so that we all have the same document in our CI and can edit it simultaneously, seeing everyone's changes in real time.

We create code to add more branches and flowers to obscure the view of our path, and we create secret compartments inside of trees at the beginning and end of the path that can hide our suits. Finally, we make a new program for trees in the surrounding area to cloud the view of our path further by increasing the amount of foliage.

Seeing Father and Mother work together is artful. Father cuts through the code with a scalpel. He adds a level of precision I couldn't hope to match...at least not yet. Mother follows every piece of Father's code and adds details to make it connect and respond to the trees in a more succinct fashion. As much as they joke about each other's shortcomings, they work phenomenally well together. It's not that Father can't be elegant, and it's very obvious that mother can create code that is efficient; but they each have a strength, and they play off each other superbly. Ari and I contribute in meaningful ways as well, but sometimes we just sit and watch for a few minutes. It's stunning.

At the end of the day, once we are done updating the code, Mother and Father send us off to reprogram all of the trees along the way to Ari's house. We are on our own because they still have their jobs to attend to. They regularly finish projects faster than expected but delay what they turn in. This allows them a free day once in a while where they can work with us and still have something to show for the day's efforts. I used to wonder how they could complete so many things in advance of the due date. After today, I understand.

CHAPTER 6
A HISTORY OF MERCED

RE: Assignment while we are gone

We are gone for the weekend for work. In our absence, write a brief history of Merced, including all major events.

Eli, comparisons to Earth are appreciated, but not necessary.

~ Eunice

A History of Merced
by Elias Jameson Hall, 724 ME

Merced Today

Merced is a planet in the Sendori galaxy. It is approximately one-third the volume of Earth, but the gravity is nearly the same as a result of a much greater density. There is one main landmass that amounts to about five percent of the landmass on Earth. Beyond that, small islands are scattered throughout the ocean. The total population is around 50,000,000 people, and it has been that way since the beginning of the Modern Era. Families have up to three children; but globally, the balance is always kept. As the population grows, family sizes reduce. As the population shrinks, families become larger. There is no law that mandates this; it is a cultural standard by which people honor the land. They do not want to ask the land for more than has already been given.

The days are thirty-six hours long. With the average lifespan being just over ninety-seven years, people on Merced live approximately eighty-four percent longer than their counterparts on Earth. The binary star system provides the planet with twenty-four hours of light each day. Three moons and a nearby planet provide enough light at night to severely mitigate the need for additional light sources outside.

Little is known about how or why souls travel from Earth to Merced, nor how those of August are chosen. The Patricians have created a narrative surrounding this, but none of it is backed up with facts—there is just a rhyme taught to children.

The Nightling Fairy

Be wary of the nightling fairy though she brings the fame
She pulls you through the void not sparing even just a name
Those who lived in service of the weak, the poor, the lame
Will find that they remember more than just from whence they came

Be wary of the silent man, he hears not what you say
His cruelty in passing life has made him just this way
The fairy brings him with the rest, treats him just the same

But he yearns for more, destroying August for the fame

Be wary of the dark woods, sons and daughters keep your clear
The rocks turn into flaming coals, the trees they turn to spears
If you hope to live beyond the edge of this day, fear
The darkened path, the smoke that howls, the smell of sulfur near

Considering the populations of Earth and Merced, it can be assumed that not all souls travel to this one planet. Specifically, the people of Merced are most likely from English speaking areas of North America. Most August Children speak English. A few have known French and Spanish as well; but English remains the official language on Merced, quelling any notion that a child of August might teach someone another tongue. Ideas abound concerning the remaining souls from Earth, but no one truly knows the answer. If any research is being done in this field it is kept a secret.

The Beginning

No one knows exactly how the people of Merced came to be. It is assumed they followed an evolutionary path, but records are hard to come by before the arrival of the Triumvirate. Any records available are subject to speculation because of how superstitious the people were.

The Triumvirate is the first recorded instance of an August Child. To be more precise, it is the first three instances. The only reason they lived was because there were three of them. Older records speak of demon possession and witchcraft. One might wonder how many August Children were executed because no one understood them. No matter the score, the history of the Modern Era of Merced begins with three: Endo Serien Oshma, Cerion Vastic Haelo and Saree Octavien Saldred.

These three children were born in the month of August to the same clan. This was the beginning of the Modern Era (ME). Not all August Children are born in the eponymous month, but they are all impressive—the meaning of august—so the name stuck.

Endo, Cerion, and Saree came into the world within days of each other. New mothers would take care of their children together. This is how the Triumvirate met. Endo shares in *The Approach of a New Dawning* that the three quickly figured out they were special. Their proximity allowed them to communicate with each other but remain hidden in plain view. They heard stories in their early days of what had come before, and they knew their lives would be in danger if they spoke a single word. Cerion had known sign language on Earth, so he taught it to Endo and Saree. They communicated this way for years without being understood by anyone but themselves. As the children grew they slowly revealed their aptitudes. They sought to protect other children who were born like them and to change the way of life for the people they grew up with. They started with food.

Clans had been mobile for as long as anyone could remember, never staying in one place more than a month. They respected the land and did not want to extend the trees beyond their abilities, saying, "We were made for the land and the land was made for us." This adage became the way of life for many people on Merced and has had lasting implications to this day. Cerion showed the people that if you cultivated and cared for a tree it would produce a near unending supply of food. The clan no longer had to move. They became the first village. Others followed suit soon after.

Endo provided vision for the future. He told the people what they could become, and so they became. He used the knowledge of the possible to direct the people towards great advances. Without his vision, Merced would not be the same place it is today. The floating vehicles on the throughways, CIs, trees made into homes; Endo's vision of the future inspired this world to become something new.

Saree helped care for the sick, but instead of instituting new practices based on her knowledge from Earth, she fully engrossed herself in the ways of the people. As time passed she helped update their methods, making small changes that others would understand. Then they would observe how the changes affected the sick and make additional adjustments as needed. Saree taught them a scientific method of improving their practices. People trusted her because she took the time to understand them. The fact that she did not speak was of little consequence. (The Silence of Saree, Bometir, 89 ME)

The Triumvirate created civilization on Merced. Everything humanity is today began with them more than 700 years ago. While it may just be a legend, those who walked on the wind had the influence to change the world.

The Uprising

After the passing of the Triumvirate, the world coalesced into a single government led by the Patricians. They were a force for goodness and peace. Everything they did was for the benefit of the people.

"For the benefit of the people," the Patricians became the ruling class. There are no elections on Merced. This single, *benevolent* group commands the masses. "For the benefit of the people," the Patricians gave August Children the option to be raised in in the capital, Suvault, for their protection. Soon, the option became a requirement. "For the safety of the August born; we protect them from the Order."

The Silent Order attacked the Patricians in Suvault. They set a building on fire. Were it not for the astonishing preparedness of the Patricians, people may have died. The Patricians are always prepared. Having known there may be pushback to their leadership, they created contingencies for every type of attack they could think of. The offenders were not caught right away, but it was discovered that the Silent Order had been behind it. After this initial discovery, it became clear that the Silent Order had been responsible for much of the mischief around the city leading up to this larger event. Their plans had been extensive, and they used a large network of people to pull it off. Not wanting to incarcerate what had grown to be a group of over a thousand people, they selected a few of the leaders who had been in charge at the time of the fire and executed them in order to set an example.

The infamy of the Silent Order led to an investigation of their origins. While the group began as a peaceful people under the watch of Saree, they desecrated her memory with their violent actions against Suvault. Now, the Silent Order is filled with those who were born deaf. Their families gave them up, knowing the evil they possessed within.

After rigorous questioning and research, we have discovered something very troubling: while the August Children were the best of humanity on Earth, the Silent Order were the worst. Their previous lives were those of evil men and women who used and abused everyone around them. They are stripped of their memory and voice in this world so their influence is limited. Even still, they are envious of August Children and anyone else in power. Just look at how they flocked to Saree. The danger they present is formidable and has caused us to react in the harshest possible way. From this day forward, everyone in the Silent

Order will be given the last name "SO," denoting their affiliation. Everyone born deaf will also be given this same name. While families are allowed to keep their children that are born deaf, they are highly encouraged to send them away to Evanwood to be with the Silent Order. Wherever they grow up, children of the Silent Order are not allowed to be educated. They may learn simple tasks in order to be productive members of society, but they cannot and will not be trained in any manner that would give them the ability to plan and execute another uprising.

Furthermore, members of the Silent Order are not to be allowed in Suvault. They will be killed on sight. We must protect those who are of August. The need for this sort of protection only serves to confirm the decision we made in bringing August Children to this city to be raised and educated. We believe the Silent Order would kill them, given the opportunity. (Address to a Unified Nation, 117 ME)

The Silent Order was no longer revered for their wisdom. They were disgraced. Families rarely moved to be with them, instead choosing to send their children who were born deaf on their own. Very few families keep these children as their own. The social stigma associated with the Order is far too strenuous for most families.

The Knowledge of the Possible

In the first century of the Modern Era, Endo and Cerion, together with Saree, told Merced of the wondrous things that had been accomplished on Earth. Trees had been harnessed for power and cultivated to grow in particular ways. Technology had been integrated with biology. Every man, woman and child came to possess a personal electronic system accessible through their own body, being visible to only themselves. Disease had been eradicated. World peace had been achieved by providing for the basic needs of every person on the planet. No one was without a home, food or water. They told everyone that people on Earth had learned to walk on the wind. Then they actually did it, or at least that is how the legend goes.

Up until the sixth century it was assumed that August Children did not arrive in chronological order, meaning—for example—that someone from the year 3000 could arrive before someone from the year 2000. This was specifically due to Endo's telling of things no one else had heard of. For centuries August Children were taught that the triumvirate were from an advanced period in Earth's history. No one had given this a second thought as it made no difference to life on Merced; but with some massive breakthroughs, questions began to arise.

For hundreds of years trees were cultivated to grow in such a way that they provided shelter. Multiple trees would be used to create rudimentary homes and small buildings. Their design was crude, but the mild climate of Merced allowed for buildings without solid walls. In 507 ME the first tree was programmed to become a different shape. Within ten years, homes across the planet were being made through programming, quickly replacing everything that had come before. Disease was severely reduced by mid sixth century; and though it has not been eradicated completely, there are now cures for nearly every ailment. In the year 575, trees were programmed to create an electronic field that could raise a combination of wood and metal off the ground. It was not the same as walking on the wind, but it served as confirmation of everything the Triumvirate had said. Taking things one step further, personal electronic systems were implanted in the first person in 598. By 625 every child was implanted with a chip by the time they were one month old.

During the seventh century August Children had many questions. They were astounded at the rate of innovation; it had never been seen before. They began to track the time periods of past lives from Earth. It was always chronological, though not necessarily in step with time on Merced. Were there a new August child every day for a year, each having died moments apart, none would arrive out of order. Endo, Cerion and Saree had not come from a time where all of these fantastic feats were possible. They lied. They dreamed. They inspired. Thus began the study of the knowledge of the possible.

I hid 25 coins in a room and I asked participants to find them all. Half of the participants were told there were there were 25, and they would find all 25 nearly every time. The mean was 24.8. The median and mode were both 25...the other half of the participants were not told how many coins there were. They would find 23, 17, 22. It varied. The mean was 21.2. The median was 20 and the mode was 19. Only 13% found all 25 coins without knowing how many there were. The knowledge of the possible is this idea that belief motivates results. If my participants believed there were 25 coins they would find all of them. Similarly, for hundreds of years people believed the things that Endo and Cerion had said were possible. Since they believed these things to be possible they would not stop until they had achieved them. Short of walking on wind, they achieved every one. The brilliance of Endo and Cerion was that they chose things in the realm of possibility and spoke so forcefully about it that no one questioned them, at least not for 500 years. (The Knowledge of the Possible, Barris, 684 ME)

Peace and Prosperity

For hundreds of years Merced has experienced relative peace and prosperity. The Patricians are nothing if not effective. That is not to say that peace came without cost. While it is required for everyone to learn English, some also learn to sign. Sign language, however, is not considered an official language by the Patricians as a means of removing the voice of the Silent Order. This is how peace is maintained.

Peace on Merced is believed to be finite. It is maintained with strict rules and order. Punishment for stepping out of line is swift and severe. "The cost of peace is never too high." Before every verdict, every punishment, every execution, these words ring in the ears of the people.

"Peace is order." This—another common axiom of the Patricians—would more accurately be represented as "Peace is orders." The peace is kept by ordering the Silent Order to stay far away and ordering August Children to remain close.

The children of August spend their formative years being trained in Suvault in whatever specialties they are interested in. Some become scientists and researchers while others become celebrities of sorts: singers, musicians, artists, actors, all of them perfect at their craft. They travel some, sharing their gifts with the people of Merced; but they always return to Suvault.

Those of August that do not become celebrities are often never heard of. Families have petitioned the Patricians for access to their children after their training is through; but the response is always the same: "August Children do not belong to the families they were born into. They have their own life, and if one wanted to reach out to their biological family on Merced he or she would do so of their own accord." But this never happens. August Children never choose to see their families as the form letter suggests they might, but this is how the peace is kept; and peace—above all other things—is worthy of any cost.

The Voice of Arielle Linivette SO

One of the most important events in the history of Merced is the voice of Arielle Linivette SO. Upon beginning her education—which happens to be illegal—she learned how to vocalize, which also happens to be illegal—or at least it would be if it was more readily known to be possible. A few weeks into her training she arrived at the home of Eunice, Isaac and Elias—which happens to make all of them criminals as well—and shared the most beautiful thing anyone has ever heard. Despite the nasal tone in her voice, this little, four-year-old girl spoke with clarity and determination.

"I am-uh Ah-Ree!"

"Arielle! That's fantastic!" Isaac said, elated with how quickly she was picking up the skill.

"No! AH-REE!" she declared with the stomp of a foot.

"You would like to be called Ari," Eunice suggested in wonder.

"Yesss!"

That was the beginning, and there is no end to what she can accomplish. No one knows her name today, aside from a select few; but she will go down as one of the greatest people in the history of Merced. This tenacious little girl with plump little cheeks and dark curly hair will be someone to be remembered.

Sources Cited

Note: all sources pulled from the "Journal of Ancient Scholars: A publication of writings from historians throughout time."

Endo Serien Oshma, “The Approach of a New Dawning”, 62 ME
Alfred Hugo Bometir, “The Silence of Saree", 89 ME
Patrician Council, “Address to a Unified Nation”, 117 ME
Haleel Escondi Barris, “The Knowledge of the Possible, an interview with Agatha Bartis Mulfer", 684 ME

Appendix

The Approach of a New Dawning

by Endo Serien Oshma, 62 ME

With my life came the new world. I am a god among men on Merced. My insight and wisdom surpass all others and I will be remembered as not just a man, but a legend.

That there were three of us was fortuitous. Alone, we may have perished, but together we were strong. Our proximity allowed us to discover that we were all special. Cerion's knowledge of sign language was an immense help. We could communicate in plain sight, undetected. For years we spent time together, talking, discussing, planning. No one knew. We hid everything until it became time for us to change everything that had come before us.

Stories had been told about sorcerers and witches and those possessed by demons. We assumed, correctly, that these were people who had been like we were, except they lacked our intuitive sense to not speak out. We did not utter a single word for over a year. We had to pretend to be the babies everyone believed we were. Saree stood as a witness of all the atrocities that had been committed. To this day, she has not uttered a single word in order to remind everyone that, despite our greatness, we were oppressed.

The declaration is now more than three decades past, but I remember it like it was yesterday. Cerion and I stood before a crowd of what must have been at least 1000 people. We told them of the future: trees being harnessed for power, technology being integrated with biology, a world without disease, peace reigning everywhere. We also promised the people they could learn how to walk on the wind. And then, in that moment, Saree joined the two of us, and in front of everyone we walked on the wind.

After this day, we promised never to walk on the wind again. We wanted to imprint this moment on the minds of the people and not dilute the power of it. We have the ability to fly, but we refrained for the sake of progress, giving people just enough to whet their appetites and believe. Others may learn to do the same thing in time, but they will have to find their own way. This was a skill we would not teach.

The power of our voices will resonate through history. We changed the course of the world. People will be amazed when they accomplish what we have outlined, but they will not be surprised; and they will remember the first voices that proclaimed these possibilities. We will live forever in the minds of the people, guiding them to greatness. We are the best of humanity and have helped to create the best humanity.

The Silence of Saree

by Alfred Hugo Bometir, 89 ME

The trials and accolades of Saree Octavien Saldred are well documented and need no further examination. What is found herein is an accounting for the silence of Saree. It is important to examine what first caused her silence and why she continues in silence to this day.

What use have words? To communicate. To converse. To inspire generations. Saree has always had words, she only expressed them in a different way. As a baby, she quickly learned the dangers of being of August, though it was not known by that name at that time. She chose not to reveal herself to anyone, save the others of the Triumvirate: Endo Serien Oshma and Cerion Vastic Haelo. This was a wise choice, and wisdom is the active choice that Saree made over and over through her lifetime.

While most children of August choose to share their experience from Earth at some point, Saree chose not to. She wanted to be judged based on the merits of who she is and not who she was. She also believed actions were louder than any words. This is why she started working with the sick. It is also, in part, why she chose silence.

Saree wanted to represent the fear that all August Children endure. Her silence was a constant reminder that she feared for her life when she was small. The only protection she had was to remain silent. She endeared herself to the people by working with the sick; not only incorporating herself, but also learning from them. She refused to teach anyone anything until she fully understood what the current practice was and how to do it. Then, and only then, she would make small changes and share them with others. It was obvious to everyone around her that she had a great depth of knowledge concerning sickness and remedies, but she never tried to force her ideas on anyone. In the same way she learned, she would teach others small things and wait for them to see how it improved upon the previous method. No one was made to do anything they didn't understand; and though she never spoke a word, everyone always understood what she was trying to do.

As time passed, people would seek out Saree to ask how they could improve various practices. Rarely would she give them a direct answer; instead, she would highlight things they did well, and then provide a few ideas they might try. It might be considered cruel to withhold information that could save a life or heal a wound faster, but Saree wanted people to learn how to improve their practice. This involved trying multiple reasonable options and then using whichever worked best in the future.

If anyone ever worked with Saree for even a few days, they would learn her favorite phrase: *Never give what can be learned; never teach, but be taught.* Saree believed the best learning came by people doing and trying on their own. Her words resonated with many people. Thus began the Silent Order.

No one ever defined what the Silent Order was, or even what it did. It just began and continued to exist. At first, a few people followed and worked with Saree and chose to be silent. Some were silent as penance for the crimes of their ancestors against August Children. Others saw the wisdom her silence provided. As years progressed the Silent Order grew into a community of over 100 people. They took in the sick and helped them. When children were born deaf it seemed a natural solution to bring them to the Order. Entire families would move to become a part of this group where they could learn how to communicate with their children and educate them. Families were not required to remain silent. Saree made sure that everyone was welcome who wanted to be a part of the community that had been built around her.

This is the history that is known

Address to a Unified Nation

Patrician Council, 117 ME

To the people of Merced,

It is with heavy hearts that we address you today. As some of you may know, the great city of Suvault was attacked earlier this week. One of our structures was burned to the ground. While we were not able to capture the offenders immediately following the event, we were able to identify and detain the leaders of the Silent Order. We are certain they were behind this unconscionable act; and we will execute them this following week, making an example for anyone who would dream of following their ways. The infamy of this group has led us to investigate their origins. While they began as a peaceful people under the watch of Saree, they now desecrate her memory with their violent actions against Suvault.

The Silent Order is filled with those who were born deaf. Their families gave them up because they knew the evil their children possessed. After rigorous questioning and research, we have discovered something very troubling: while the August Children were the best of humanity on Earth, the Silent Order were the worst. Their previous lives were those of evil men and women who used and abused everyone around them. They are stripped of their memory and voice in this world so their influence is limited. Even still, they are envious of August Children and anyone else in power. Just look at how they flocked to Saree. The danger they present is formidable and has caused us to react in the harshest possible way. From this day forward, everyone in the Silent Order will be given the last name "SO," denoting their affiliation. Everyone born deaf will also be given this same name. While families are allowed to keep their children that are born deaf, they are highly encouraged to send them away to Evanwood to be with the Silent Order. Wherever they grow up, children of the Silent Order are not allowed to be educated. They may learn simple tasks in order to be productive members of society, but they cannot and will not be trained in any manner that would give them the ability to plan and execute another uprising.

Furthermore, members of the Silent Order are not to be allowed in Suvault. They will be killed on sight. We must protect those who are of August. The need for this sort of protection only serves to confirm the decision we made in bringing August Children to this city to be raised and educated. We believe the Silent Order would kill them, given the opportunity.

These measures may seem severe, but it is for the benefit of the people of Merced. We must protect the peace and unity that has been created. This merciless assault, this uprising of the Silent Order will not be tolerated. We do not believe that children should be held responsible for the actions of their past lives, so we will not execute them. Instead we will allow them to live in isolation. The Silent Order will have no voice in this world. They will have no ability to communicate with the Patricians on any matter. They will be cut off from society, a blight against our otherwise perfect world. In this way, we grant them mercy.

When we detained the leaders of the Silent Order, we found plans for several more attacks on Suvault as well as attacks on individual villages. While we believe that we have removed any possibility of a future threat, we will keep a watchful eye on every area they had identified. Vigilant citizens of our illustrious nation should be keenly aware of the danger that surrounds them. If you see something that concerns you, do not remain silent. Words—spoken aloud—have power. Words have more power than waving your hands about. Words have more power than silence. Words contain generations of wisdom. Silence only hides the truth. It is deceptive. It is envious. It hungers for power.

Good people, be deceived no longer. Reject those who would choose silence. Peace begets peace. Silence begets destruction.

The Knowledge of the Possible

"An Interview With Agatha Bartis Mulfer"

Haleel Escondi Barris, 684 ME

Q: First things first, can you tell me a little bit about who you are?

A: Of course. My name is Agatha Bartis Mulfer. I work at the university in Selter. I conduct research. In this case—the reason I believe you're here to see me—my research concerns the knowledge of the possible.

Q: Tell me about the work you did on the knowledge of the possible.

A: I hid 25 coins in a room and I asked participants to find them all. Half of the participants were told there were there were 25, and they would find all 25 nearly every time. The mean was 24.8. The median and mode were both 25. Do I need to explain the differences?

Q: No, you're fine. A little technical language never hurt anyone. Please continue.

A: Well, the other half of the participants were not told how many coins there were. They would find 23, 17, 22. It varied. The mean was 21.2. The median was 20 and the mode was 19. Only 13% found all 25 coins without knowing how many there were. The knowledge of the possible is this idea that belief motivates results. If my participants believed there were 25 coins they would find all of them. Similarly, for hundreds of years people believed the things that Endo and Cerion had said were possible. Since they believed these things to be possible they would not stop until they had achieved them. Short of walking on wind, they achieved every one. The brilliance of Endo and Cerion was that they chose things in the realm of possibility and spoke so forcefully about it that no one questioned them, at least not for 500 years.

Q: What is the legacy of Endo and Cerion, and to a lesser extent, Saree? Are they liars? Are they legends?

A: Well, they are legends for sure; and I don't think they will be remembered as liars. I think they will be remembered as visionaries. Discovering that they lied doesn't change the way people view them very much. It just shows how much vision they had.

Q: In all the trials you did with your study, what was the most remarkable thing that happened?

A: Once, on accident, I told someone there were 26 coins in the room. They found 26. I don't know how. I thought I had checked the room thoroughly, but evidently not. A single trial doesn't prove anything, but to me it cemented everything my research had been telling me up to that point. Hundreds of people had come through before this. No one had found that 26th coin. No one believed it existed. Once someone believed, they found it.

Q: That is a powerful anecdote, especially when backed with your other work. What made you choose this coin experiment?

A: I wanted to do something that could be tested in a short amount of time. I didn't exactly have 500 years to see if my theories were correct. This was a simple experiment, but it held the same philosophy of Endo and Cerion.

Q: How did you run the experiment? Did people know what you were testing them on?

A: No, I think that would have disrupted the data. So we lied! I'm telling you, we could not have modeled this any better. When someone came in we would tell them to find all the coins and that they were being timed, but we couldn't tell them why. We insisted they shouldn't rush and instead be thorough. Half of the subjects were not told how many coins were in the room, the other half were.

Q: And how many subjects did you test?

A: With the help of my research assistants, 3000 over the course of a few weeks.

Q: Do you feel that your research proves this theory of the knowledge of the possible?

A: I think it adds to the growing voice on the subject. We see over and over how different experiments are showing that knowledge and belief lead to greater, previously inconceivable outcomes.

Q: Given the results of your research, how do you feel about the lies that Endo and Cerion told?

A: Are they lies if every one of them turned out to be true here on Merced?

Q: That's a fair question that I don't have the answer to. How do you feel about the Patrician policy to withhold information about Earth?

A: I think there is a fair argument to be made for what they claim, but I am hesitant to accept that as their true purpose.

Q: Explain what you mean.

A: The Patricians have told us the reason they withhold information about Earth is to spur innovation. They want to act as Endo and Cerion did and inspire new inventions and creations. The theory is that if we do not know what was possible on Earth then we will not be constrained by it. The problem I have with this thinking is that we all know what they are doing. If Endo and Cerion had told us they lied we would not have come this far this fast. Also, this is the most recent explanation given to us by the Patricians, but they have been withholding information about Earth for centuries. This makes me think they have kept their true motives hidden. I don't know what their reasons are, so I have no idea if it is good for the people or bad. Given the option, I would have information about Earth released to everyone. I think it would be a windfall for the scientific community.

Q: One last question for you, do you think we will ever walk on the wind?

A: One last question for you, do you believe in fairy tales? It is generally understood that the people of Merced were very superstitious up until the arrival of the Triumvirate. The existence of August Children likely caused these superstitions; but without knowing how things were happening, every small strange thing was attributed to mystical powers. There's an old story from Earth, one of few I've heard: the Salem witch trials. It's about how people were accused of witchcraft and executed for their supposed crimes. Our history is fraught with similar stories, which we now know relate to those of August. In Salem, they only executed twenty people. I don't even want to venture a guess as to how many people died here. Either way, superstition is superstition. People will believe whatever they want, no matter what planet they are born on. They will think they saw something that they didn't. Someone will tell a story and embellish the truth. I have seen men and women manipulate the wind in small ways—the garafin allows us that—but nothing more than I could accomplish with a large fan to wave around. I am certain that Endo, Cerion and Saree were a marvel to behold, but I don't believe anyone ever has or ever will walk on the wind. It is a legend, a myth, a fable.

Q: With an attitude like that you'll never learn to walk on the wind. Of course, I jest.

A: I think the problem we encounter is that some things seem impossible and some things are impossible. Our transportation seemingly flies through the air. I'll count that as close enough.

Q: That seems more than fair. Those are all the questions I have today. Thank you for speaking with me and sharing your insights.

A: My pleasure. Thank you for having me.

CHAPTER 7
GARAFIN

RE: Elias Jameson Hall Test Scores 5YO

The child scores in the 90th percentile or higher in every category. The most surprising score was his social awareness: 95th percentile. The reason this is surprising is because his family seems to live in isolation. I know Jameson and Hall are well respected in their fields, and they must have friends; but the logs show that no one visits them and only on rare occasion do they visit others. Obviously, the child is not of August, but he is exceptionally bright. Unfortunately, this means we have no recourse against the family for choosing to homeschool him as long as his scores stay so high. I guess it's not wholly surprising since his parents are so well educated, but still, it's suspicious. I would have liked to have access to the additional battery of "assessments" students are given in primary school. I think the boy may be an exceptional candidate to be a Patrician.

~ Garrison

RE: RE: Elias Jameson Hall Test Scores, 5YO

Time is on our side. If the boy is suited to our line of work we can help direct him that way at university. I, too, was hoping he wouldn't do so well at home. But we will find another way.

~ Ward

I haven't been up this early in quite some time; have to get out of the house as quickly as I can. I haven't seen Ari for two days. This is far too long. Mother and Father share the unfortunate disposition that Ari should not come over while they are gone; they got back last night. Two steps out the door and I fly. Not literally. I just run very fast to get to the tree that holds my suit. A few buckles and I'll be ready to literally fly. Vest. Helmet. Chaps. One last buckle! A single jump and I am—

"Good morning!" She beat me. She's so happy she beat me. She can't stop smiling. She's not even trying to disguise her smug superiority.

"You know, had you left at any reasonable time this morning I would have gotten to *your* place before you left."

"Oh yes," the sarcasm flows out of Ari's mouth, "if things had happened differently this morning I'm certain the outcome would have changed." One of the benefits of being around my parents all the time is that we have learned how to be awful to each other in the most amusing ways. "Race?"

"Of course!" We can't actually race. Our path only allows for single file flying, but we fly as fast as we can. At the halfway mark, we stop. A large oak stands off to the side, twice the diameter of any tree nearby. The gap in the trunk of the tree looks like a deformity. It isn't more than twenty-five centimeters wide, but when entered sideways, it becomes clear that it spirals inward. The further in, the wider the gap, until finally a narrow staircase appears, leading down, following the outer wall of the tree. As we travel down the stairs the space becomes larger until we stand in a cylindrical room just over three meters in diameter. No outside light penetrates the walls, but we programmed small dahlias to hang from the ceiling, each providing a light that matches the color of its petals. We never designed any furniture, and the staircase is a little wonky, but we love it. It's our own design—one of our first—and it's perfect. We sit in the middle of the floor, as is our tradition.

"So where's the food?" Ari places an expectant palm in front of me.

"You thought I brought food? Some of us ate breakfast in our homes instead of rushing out the door just to beat the other."

She gives me a skeptical sideways glance. "So where's the food?"

"I told you already, I—"

"Elias, I've seen you skip breakfast so you can edit a tiny piece of boring code. I am the best friend you've ever had on this entire planet and you haven't seen me for two whole days! Do you really expect me to believe that you ate breakfast this morning before you left to see me? You really need to learn how to lie better."

I think about fighting it, but every word she said is true. "The wisdom of Saree lies with the deaf." I hand Ari a piece of fruit as I bite into another.

"You know they mean that as an insult now, right? And you expect me to take this food from you after you have so deeply hurt me?" She takes a very large bite and muffles threw her chewing, "I am offended, sir, that you would treat a young girl in such a way."

We sit in silence as we finished our food, just enjoying each other's company. Time passes quickly and we set out for home. We come into the house at the perfect moment; Mother and Father just finished preparing breakfast.

"Isaac, do you think that being deaf has heightened Ari's sense of smell, or is it that those of August have a special ability to know when breakfast is on the table?"

"Oh, I think they programmed our home long ago to send out a signal when someone starts cooking."

"You can do that?" Ari says with a mouth full of bread. Everyone laughs.

The truth is that Mother and Father make breakfast at the same exact time every day. Ari and I are very good at keeping track of time, or at least we are good at setting a timer on our CIs.

Mother doesn't waste any more time before jumping right into things. "We read both of your papers. Eli, yours was good, though your thinly veiled cynicism was a little *too* thinly veiled at some points; but you covered all the content well enough."

"I knew they wouldn't like how cynical yours was," Ari says with a smug grin.

"I knew it too, but the instructions were very minimal and did not require me to hide my true feelings."

"So you're a stickler for rules now?" Father chuckles to himself. "That sounds very much like you. 'Eli the rule follower' is what I always say." Father doesn't actually care about what I had done. Neither does Mother. They always critique my work to make sure I know what issues there might be with it. Next time I won't be so cynical. Maybe I'll just throw in some idioms from Earth they won't understand.

"Ari," Mother continues, "yours was very good. I particularly appreciated the connection you feel to Saree. I could see that you admire her very much."

"She was silent like me. Or at least like I used to be." Her grin nearly eclipses her face.

"Excellent. You should be proud to be associated with Saree. She was wise and so are you."

"Something we noticed in both of your papers," Father says, "is a lack of knowledge about Garafin. It is a very prominent part of what makes Merced so special, though it isn't understood by many people. We realized that we have not discussed it enough, so that's what we are going to talk about today."

Once finished eating, Father beckons us into the living room for a lesson. "Garafin is an element found in nearly everything on Merced," he begins. "It is my understanding it does not exist on Earth..." He pauses and looks at me.

"I never memorized the periodic table, but I'm fairly sure it's not on there. I don't ever remember hearing of it."

"Good enough for me." He flashes a quick smile and continues. "On Merced, Garafin is found in the air and in the trees and nearly everywhere else you can think of. Concentrated amounts have even been injected into your fingertips, which allows you to interact with your CI. The reason the pods can float is because Garafin acts similarly to a magnet when manipulated properly. The trees produce a positive charge constantly. The pods are also given a positive charge. The reason the pods are made of metal as well as wood is because the metal helps hold the charge for longer. Eventually, even with the metal, the charge eventually returns to a neutral state and it is no longer able to float until it has been given a new charge. One of the reasons you have to store your suits in a tree is so they can use some of the power from the tree to build up the proper charge."

"Why haven't other people made suits to fly?" Ari asks.

"A few things about that. First, the Patricians control all the pods. No one is allowed to use the throughway with any mechanism of their own design, though few could actually pull that off. It started as a safety protocol, but I imagine there are other motives behind it. No matter the case, it's simple enough to go anywhere you want. Just call on a pod to come, input directions, and you're off. Very few people have ever had need of a different means of transport. Second, I wouldn't quite use the term 'fly.' The pods can't go above the trees or into clearings. They really just float on the throughways. I know it's a small distinction, but I'm here to make sure you learn every little detail. But back to your question. No one has made a suit, or really even thought of making one, because things like that aren't allowed on the throughways. No one has made their own path because they aren't as capable as the two of you. Sure, Euny and I helped, but what we added was more about optimization and remaining hidden than about functionality. There is no law that specifically prohibits what you have done, but that is probably due to a lack of imagination. The truth, though, is that most people don't need a special path. Being of the Silent Order, Ari, has meant that you can't call a pod to take you places. You can accompany others, but can't go alone. Most people don't have that problem and never have a need for anything more than what is provided already.

"Each of you are mature in your own way, but your youthful bodies give you different ideas about playing and fun than an adult would have. There may be other children who dream of making a flying suit, but none of them have the capacity to do it; and by the time they are adults they no longer see the need."

"Shouldn't it be a 'floating' suit?" The emphasis on the word "floating" embellishes Ari's mocking tone.

"I had to reconsider. I wanted to make sure you knew what was technically happening, but I don't think any child dreams of floating...just flying. So, however improper it may be, you are the proud owner of a flying suit." Father is still a little boy on the inside; and though he won't make his own, he will always revel in the joy of our flying suits.

"Continuing on, Garafin is also what allows you to interact with your CI. While you don't have much in your fingers, it is more concentrated than what is in the air. Our bodies also hold charges, though not anything close to what the pods hold; but this charge allows the CI to identify your finger movements in three dimensions."

"If our bodies have small charges, is it possible to float without a suit?" I'm positive it wouldn't be practical, but I don't need something to be practical to have fun.

"That's a good question. The short answer is no. The charge we hold isn't enough to counteract the weight of our bodies, but let me show you what you can do. Please understand I have been practicing at this for many years. I'm certain you will both pick it up faster than me, but it will take time and practice." He moves to the center of the room. "Depending on various conditions around us, our bodies may hold a positive or negative charge, so to speak. The air, when unaffected by anything else, will have no charge. If you can successfully expel your charge you can...well...just let me show you."

Breathing in deeply with his eyes closed, Father raises his elbows to shoulder height. With his hands out front he makes a circle with each in opposing directions. As each hand completes the revolution, his arms raise up as if he is conducting an orchestra into a crescendo, only to have them come crashing down to his waist immediately after. His entire body recoils to a more natural position, and at this moment a gust of wind swirls around Father's feet and expels outwards until it dissipates completely. Both Ari and I feel the tiny blast on our ankles. It wasn't just the motion of his arms that created this; Father shifted the wind.

"Do it again!" Our voices ring out in one accord.

Father laughs heartily. "I won't be able to do it again for some time. My charge is depleted. It will have to build up over the next few hours before I'll have enough to go again."

"Is this how the Triumvirate walked on the wind?" I can barely contain the words in my mouth.

"If they *did* walk on the wind, I would guess this had something to do with it."

"Do you think that since Saree started the Silent Order and I'm part of the Silent Order that I could walk on the wind? I mean, I know I'm not a child of August; but that shouldn't stop me, right?" Ari's excitement has her talking faster than me. Her speech is improving every day; speed is the latest development.

"I would hope that the two of you would surpass my skills, but the amount of charge you'd need, and for how long you'd have to sustain it—"

Ari cuts in, "It's fine, we'll figure it out."

"Yup, I definitely believe the Triumvirate walked on the wind, and so will we!"

"That's what the knowledge of the possible is all about, right?"

"That's exactly what I was thinking!" We are of one mind.

"We're kids, and kids are great at suspending disbelief. Better than adults. We'll just ignore all the science that says it's not possible."

"The science doesn't matter anyway because it *is* possible."

Father is laughing so hard he has to sit down. Ari and I are a machine with the same mission, drive and purpose. Gathering himself, Father offers us some help. "Would you like to practice the motions with me?"

Both of us nod in silence. We don't want our words to delay anything. Father starts to laugh again but stops himself with some deep, calming breaths. He models the motion for us slowly. We copy him perfectly. He shows us full speed. Again, we match his movement in every aspect. Neither one of us create any gusts of wind, but we don't care. Father understands exactly how fast we learn. He told us it would take time and practice to master it. While we experience minor disappointment on our first try, there is no lack of resolve. We trust him fully. We are not phased in the least.

For twenty more minutes, the three of us practice together. Father makes minor corrections to our form, or offers suggestions on how our small bodies might better accomplish certain things. We commit every minute detail to memory.

"I think this is plenty of new information for today," Father tells us. "Would you like to go practice in your secret hideout?"

"How do you know about our secret hideout?"

Ari jabs me in the side with her elbow. Through clenched teeth, speaking out of the side of her mouth, she whispers, "You're not supposed to confirm or deny any mention of an ecret-say ideout-hay." The tone and inflection are perfect.

Mother pops her head around a corner so she can see us. "The two of you leave the house for hours at a time. You are youthful and creative. You also happen to be the most skilled children I have ever known. If you don't have a secret hideout by now I will be *severely* disappointed in you."

We never intended to keep our fort a secret from my parents. In truth, we were quite certain they could find it with ease if they ever needed to. Mother would recognize the design immediately as it was a failed project that had given us the idea in the first place. It's fun to have a secret, though. It's also fun that Mother and Father allow us the pretense of keeping our secret.

We let our sheepish grins speak for us and bolt for the kitchen. We stock up on food since we have no intention of returning for lunch. Once fully loaded, we set out.

We spend the rest of the day in our secret fort practicing what Father had shown us. For the first few hours we move through everything at a snail's pace, correcting each other and making small adjustments until we are sure we have mastered every movement to perfection. Then full speed over and over and over again. We expect nothing, so there is no dismay when, at the end of the day, we have not shifted any air. We will continue to practice. We are not deterred. One day, we will walk on the wind just as Endo, Cerion and Saree did.

CHAPTER 8
GONE

RE: Elias Jameson Hall Test Scores 7YO

The boy passed his tests again…with nearly identical scores. Shockingly identical. If we didn't administer the test ourselves I would say his parents were helping him cheat somehow. I do believe the identical scores could give us a reason to bring him in for "additional" testing. We could run a standard battery for his age and get a clearer idea of his trajectory. I doubt his parents would object since they likely wouldn't want to ruffle any feathers, so to speak. Please advise.

~ Garrison

RE: Elias Jameson Hall Test Scores 7YO

Hold off for now. I agree that they would not protest, but it could tip our hand. They will be more likely to make a mistake if we leave them alone. I know it can be frustrating to wait, but it is the right call for the time being.

Be aware, I catalog all of our correspondence in their files. Nothing you're doing is going to waste and all of it will contribute to their ultimate demise. They are either hiding something or they are the dumbest smart people I have ever encountered.

~ Ward

Ari is never late. For the last two years we have met in our hideout nearly every morning to practice shifting the wind—two hours every day. It's not the only time we spend practicing, but it is consistent. We are committed to learning this skill. Having a consistent time to practice has been a huge help. Two hours is just enough: we have a charge when we arrive so we can immediately practice the move Father taught us; we eat a small snack to tide us over until breakfast, and then we work on creating new moves to try once our charge is built up again.

The mornings are our favorite time of day. Sure, we learn plenty the rest of the day; and none of it would be considered bad, but we are bound and determined to walk on the wind. Our skills are close to matching Father's, and we've had small success with other motions. Our current theory is that there must be some motions that harness our charge better than others. Higher efficiency is the goal. It doesn't seem like efficiency alone will be enough, but it's a good place to start. Once we find something that works better we will make plans on our next step.

I'm not any better at shifting than Ari is. Really, in everything we do, the only advantage I have on her is my prior knowledge. She's learning everything from scratch. She is exceptionally intelligent, creative and fiercely competitive. I'm not certain if she actually cares who wins, though she *will* hold it over my head when she does. What she truly wants is someone who can challenge her and help her become better. That is a large part of who we are to each other. But she's not here. I have to grab food on my way out the door in the morning, so she beats me here more often than I beat her. The most I have ever won by is ten minutes. It's been thirty.

Something is wrong. I quickly gather my things and put my suit back on. Within ten minutes I reach Ari's end of the path. I leave my suit on in case I need to make a quick escape. I check the tree for Ari's; it's still there. She hasn't even made it this far. I have never been in her house, but I know exactly where it is. I start making my way.

From twenty meters out I can see that there is no activity in the house. No lights. Nobody moving around. The back door is open. Did they leave? Did she go without saying goodbye? My entire body prickles with fear. She's the only friend I have. There are three people on this entire planet whom I love. I cannot bear to lose any of them.

I approach the back door slowly, holding a duality of thoughts and emotions at the ready. Care, concern, worry, anxiety—that's how I feel. But also at the ready is the selfish rage of a spoiled seven-year-old boy who has been severely inconvenienced by the late arrival of the help. If her parents are home I will need the latter to explain my presence. It's possible that no one is home. I don't have anything prepared for that, but no one will be watching me in that case.

Standing at the back of the house, I'm close enough to interface with the home's console. I quickly send a message to Mother and Father to let them know what's going on. I knock on the back door as it swings gently in the morning breeze.

"Hello? Is anybody home?" Someone is here. Someone has to be here. She can't be gone. I can't lose her. Not now. I won't believe it's true.

Just like home, the kitchen is at the back of the house. I step inside and look around. Nothing. I move to the right and follow the path of the curved wall as it leads me to the dining room and then the living room. My heart stops for a moment. Ari is laying in the middle of the floor, motionless and silent.

Emotional state number one. I see no sign of her parents. In fact, I don't see any evidence that they live here at all; the house is empty. I kneel next to Ari and place my hand on her back to let her know I'm here. She looks up at me, tears welled up in her eyes.

"I came as fast as I could. Are you ok? What happened?"

With considerable effort, she sits up and leans into me. I'm smaller than she is by a good measure, but size is not a determining factor in being comforted. She leans her head on my shoulder and hands me a piece of paper. It's a note.

Arielle,

As you know, we loved you very much. When your father and I found out I was pregnant we were overjoyed. It was one of the happiest times of our lives. Meeting you for the first time is one of the memories I cherish the most in this life. You were beautiful and perfect, at least as far as we knew. I loved you so very much on that day.

It was difficult for us when we found out that you were of the Silent Order. You probably don't remember, but we fought for weeks over whether to keep you or send you away. I couldn't bear to see you go. I knew you weren't perfect in your last life—more than likely you were quite awful—but you were so cute and precious in this life. It didn't seem right.

We had considered sending you away again when you were four. We thought it would be best, but then another gift came…you began to work for a family that desperately needed help. They would never love you, but it would give you a greater purpose in life than living with all the other murderers and rapists and war criminals in the Silent Order. I was still concerned with your behavior as you grew, but this was a situation that might teach you what a healthy life is like. I had hoped it would help you learn how to be a functional member of society, something I was sure the Order could not teach you.

For years we have struggled through life, having become social pariahs because we kept you. We have no friends. No one is willing to be associated with a family that has a child like you. Our jobs are nearly always in jeopardy because of you. The people we work with found out about you and the smallest errors in our performance have resulted in demotions, less pay, and isolation. No one wants to work together with us. They are worried they will lose their jobs along with us. It's very difficult to be the parents of a deaf girl. You cannot imagine how it grates on us every day.

I have repeatedly told your father that we cannot leave you, that it would be cruel to send you away. He always relented. We would keep you. Then you created a problem: I noticed you had been breaking the law. It is forbidden for children of the Silent Order to be educated. It started with small things. You had learned a few new words. Your form when signing improved. I had assumed it was just because you were communicating with other people on a more regular basis. Those things should improve with time. Then I noticed that you seemed to follow verbal conversations your father and I were having. Over the next few months I dropped in little bits of information when speaking that I did not share when signing with you. I wouldn't have been able to catch it except that I am with you every day: you have learned to read lips. I cannot imagine the punishment for someone of the Silent Order who is learning as you are, but we can no longer be party to it.

I don't know where you're learning things, but I do know that you have been leaving earlier and returning later as time has progressed. It's very selfish of you to have acted in this way. I am hurt and dismayed. I have not told the family you work for, nor do I know what repercussions this could have on your father and I; but please understand that you have endangered everyone around you. When you were born, I never could have dreamed the problems you would create for us and how selfish you would be.

We considered sending you to Evanwood now, but we decided you might view yourself as the victim in that scenario if we forced you to go. Certainly, the Patricians will find you and send you, helping you understand your place in this world. Your father and I need to start a new life, because everyone here knows about you; so we left. I won't share where we have gone because we don't want you to try and follow us. You have ruined our lives enough. Please understand that we are the victims here. You are the one who has pushed us out. You have forced us to leave our homes and our jobs. I did love you once, and I thought that you had loved us, but it is obvious to me now that you are not capable of love. If you have any affection left for us you will refrain from sharing our names with anybody or associating yourself with us in any way.

I can only hope that this circumstance will teach you a lasting lesson. You're so eager to learn, maybe you'll actually learn something from this. And again, you've put me in an insufferable position—making me party to your crime—having to teach you a lesson. I should not have had to do this. I should not have trusted you when you were a baby, looking so beautiful and innocent. I am sorry I allowed myself a moment of hope those eleven years ago. Please forgive me that error in judgement. Today, we remedy that mistake. We have not contacted the authorities directly, but they will come. Please do not do anything that could jeopardize our safety any further.

Sincerely,

Mother and Father

They are repugnant. Just by reading the letter I can taste their vile, decrepit lies on my tongue. It's amazing that such a beautiful and kind soul came from people who are so monstrous. Deep breaths. Now is not the time to be angry—I need to offer compassion.

"You found this when you came home last night?"

She nods.

"And you've been here alone since then?"

Again, she nods.

"I'm sorry I wasn't here for you sooner." I would have cried on the floor with her all night if I would have known.

Ari rarely speaks of her parents. I believe they care about her in some twisted, perverted sense; and I believe that she loves them despite all their flaws. In the last seven years, she has slowly grown away from them as she built a new family with us, but she still loves them. They are still her parents. They made the choice to keep her and not send her away. They are the reason she was able to learn and grow. She might have never known them. She might have grown up with others in the Order.

We sit in silence for a half hour. Then, a light knock comes from the front door. Mother and Father are here. Without any invitation, or any sound at all, they come in. Seeing the situation in front of them they immediately understand and sit down on the floor next to us. They don't say anything. There is nothing to be said.

"We need to gather your things and go." Mother's tone is both matter of fact and calming. It could be dangerous if we stay too long. This needs to look like my parents made a short visit.

Mother follows Ari into her room to help her grab a few things. Father and I scour the rest of the house to make sure everything looks exactly as it should. How exactly should it look? Mostly, I try to make sure things don't look out of place. Shut the back door, put away errant dishes, shuffle around aimlessly, try to understand how someone could do this to Ari.

I still have the letter. I fold it and place it in my pocket. I have no idea if Ari will want to keep it or not. Either way, it can't be found here.

Ari emerges from her room with a small bag, presumably filled with clothes and a few personal effects. The four of us gather in the living room. We look at each other in silence as if to say that we all completed our assigned tasks. We are done. Walking out the front door we see the pod my parents arrived in. We all climb in and are on our way.

"Where are we going?" Ari asks, still in a daze. She can't think beyond the next step she takes, much less her entire future.

"Home." It is the most reassuring thing Mother could say. It's inclusive and permanent. I'm not sure Ari grasps the fullness of it, but it's enough. Upon arriving, it becomes clear. There is a new door next to my own.

"We never wanted to presume anything, and we didn't know what would happen; but we also wanted to be prepared." Father's voice wavers a little as he tries to explain. "We didn't want to take you from your family, and we had no idea they would leave. We just thought that there might be a need at some point. We designed and made this room a few years ago. We added the door to it today. If you would have us, we would like you to be a permanent part of our family."

Sign language has the benefit of being able to speak amidst a vast array of tears. Even still, "Thank you!" is all Ari can get out. She wraps her arms around Mother and Father as best she can in a hug that lasts far longer than either of them expected.

The room is nearly identical to mine. How did I not notice it was here?

"We added it to your mother's closet," Father whispers in my ear, answering the question he can see written on my face. "She'll have to downsize some," he jests, "but I think she'll manage."

There isn't much to it—a bed, some drawers, a window—but we have never needed much to begin with. We have each other and that is plenty for now.

***

It doesn't take long for us to settle into our new routine. Ari and I still go to our hideout every morning to practice. It's good for us to get out of the house and be active. The sting of Ari's parents leaving diminishes each day. After a week passes she decides to burn the letter, and we hold a little ceremony just outside of our fort.

Our morning of practice is almost over. We've been practicing the same move for the last few days and gave it one last attempt earlier this morning when we first arrived. Two hours later and we are outside, huddled around the scraps of parchment Ari had ripped up.

"Do you want to say any last words?" We are treating this as a funeral of sorts. She doesn't expect to see them ever again.

"I wouldn't really know what to say."

"Tell me about them. What do you remember?"

"I remember everything. I didn't have language, but I remember parts of the day I was born. I was a bit lost for the first month—conscious thought is strange when you don't have any words to describe things to yourself—but once they discovered I was of the Silent Order my mother picked up a book and started to learn sign language. I learned quickly. As soon as I could move myself, I began to look through the book to learn things on my own. I surpassed my mother's abilities within the first six months. She knew it, too. My father hated me most of the time, but my mother...she was conflicted. She loved me with all her heart and hated everything I was at the same time. She kept it a secret that I was learning. Really, she just pretended not to know. It eased her conscience. She's the only reason I'm here, though.

"I remember the fights they had about me. Obviously, I couldn't hear what they were saying, nor did I know how to read their lips; but I could see the anger in their faces as they yelled and screamed and pointed at me. They assumed their deaf child wouldn't hear a thing, forgetting that body language often tells more than words. I could also feel the vibrations as my father would stomp up the stairs, feet heavy with exasperation, and then the rattle as he slammed the door to his study. It was awful, but I was alive.

"I didn't know what I was to them until I was two years old. I knew I was despised, but I didn't know why. I begged my mother to tell me and she finally gave in. It's a wicked thing to tell your only daughter that she is worthless and broken. She cried as she told me, as if saying it hurt her as much as it hurt me. I had never done anything to deserve being treated this way. I tried to tell her that. She just kept on telling me that I was young and didn't understand. So, I committed myself to learning everything I could. I had to understand. It had been made clear to me that I was not to be educated as any normal child would be, so I was on my own.

"I taught myself to read. I convinced my mother that I wanted books to look at the pictures. Then I played my part and always showed her the prettiest pictures with the brightest colors. By three years old they would leave me at home by myself as they went to work. I would go into my father's study and read for hours on end. It was difficult at first, but a constant flow of new picture books helped me learn enough words that I began to be able to discern meaning from context. When I was four my father came home early one day and found me reading in the study. It was a crime, and he wanted to give me up immediately. Again, they fought. This time I could feel the reverberation of every word, every insult, every snide remark. My father was desperate to be rid of me, and my mother could not bear it. I think they would have sent me away if not for your mother, Eli.

"I was at the market when I met Eunice. I would have searched for her sooner if I knew that such a person existed. She was kind and compassionate to me when others were not. I decided that this was my only escape. I knew it was risky, but I had to ask someone to teach me. She was the first person in this entire world to show me any attention without thinking I was some kind of monster on the inside. This was my only shot, so I asked her to take me to her house and then begged her to teach me. I believe you know the story from there."

"Your mother loved you. She didn't know how to do it very well, but she loved you."

"I know. Without her I would have been lost."

With that, we hunch down, blocking the breeze from the small mound of parchment; and we set it on fire. We both stand. I place my hands together and plunge them down towards the small flame, as if I am about to dive into water. A swift separation sends the wind down into the center, dividing the embers. Smoke and ash spread to make a circle around the two of us, slowly rising in the air. That is all the charge I have. It's Ari's turn. She holds her hands in front of her chest as she breathes in deeply. With a violent exhale, she sends her hands towards the ground and out away from her body. The gust of wind causes every last piece hanging in the air to fully ignite and burn up. Black particles linger in the air around us for a moment and then slowly move with the wind to become a part of the earth again. This is the most meaningful thing we have ever done with shifting the wind. It is perfect.

It hadn't felt right earlier this morning to fly to the ceremony. Today is about catharsis and walking is better suited to that. Now that the event is over, we head home.

"I am amazed that you remember so much from so young, but you can't remember anything from before."

"I can't remember my past life, but I remember the void."

"Wait, what?" It had never come up before. I had incorrectly assumed it was something that only August Children experience.

"I remember the void. Not much of it, but I remember standing alone amongst many. I guess I wasn't exactly standing. Brilliant colors rushed by, but I remained still...focused. I imagine it like a sea of diamonds and flowers, each of their own kind, every color reflecting a thousand times over; but that was only secondary. My main focus was on a distant light in the dark. Beyond the sea there was only darkness save this one spot, and it wasn't even light—it wasn't bright enough. It barely held any color at all, but it was beautiful. It was the coming of a new day, or maybe the leaving of an old day, or maybe both. I felt connected to it. I wanted to go to it. And that's the last thing I remember before meeting my mother."

"That sounds beautiful. Thank you for sharing with me."

I recount own experience in the void and we discuss, at length, the meaning of the light, or lack thereof, in the distance. Wild guesses of the uneducated—concerning a topic that very few know about and no one has the ability to study—result in very little. But we enjoy sharing this common memory. It makes each of us feel a little less alone in the world.

Walking brings us home late. We left earlier than normal this morning, but we are still a few minutes off. We aren't excited about being late for breakfast, but it seemed fair to assume Mother and Father might wait for us; or at the very least, save us some food. I open the door and hear a new voice. I stretch my arm in front of Ari and sign, "Extreme caution." We slink into the kitchen where we can't be seen, and I begin to sign everything I can hear so Ari can know what's going on as well.

"The house was abandoned," the strange voice says. "It's not too uncommon for parents to leave children of the Silent Order, but we have to follow up to find where they are and send them to live with their people. Our logs show that you visited their house a few days ago." The pregnant pause says he's done, as if he's asked a question.

"We have used her as a house maid and caretaker for our son for years now. She didn't show up one morning, so we went to check on things. No one was home." The unsteady nature of Mother's voice tells me she isn't sure what to say. We hadn't made a specific plan for how to deal with this situation. I had assumed Mother and Father had planned something and would fill us in soon, but that is clearly not the case. None of us are prepared. It is most certainly a Patrician in the other room and it will be hard to keep our stories straight. This is dangerous territory.

Ari nudges me with her elbow and instructs me to run into the living room and proclaim our return. Obviously, I need to act like a boy of seven. We have never had a Patrician in our house before—everything needs to be perfect.

"We're home from our morning walk!"

"You didn't tell me she was *still* working for you!" The Patrician is upset. This isn't good.

"We were in the process of explaining." Father is stalling and glances at Ari. "We will gladly share everything we know with you."

"Actually," the Patrician continues, "there isn't anything further I need. You people seem nice enough, and it hasn't been that long. I'll just to take her away with me and that will be the end of it. They can figure out what to do with her in Evanwood."

Ari looks at Mother inquisitively, as if she has no idea what is going on. Mother signs, knowing the Patrician cannot, "Ari, he wants to take you away. I wish you would have stayed hidden. I'm not sure what we can do at this point, but we will figure something out."

Ari loses control of herself. Sheer panic fills her eyes. She looks directly at the Patrician and starts waving her arms wildly.

"I have no idea what she's trying to say." He looks more annoyed than anything. "Can someone please translate this...mess?"

Mother asks Ari to slow down a little bit and then relays everything Ari says. It is a masterful performance.

"I don't want to go to the Silent Order. I don't want to live with those vile people! This family has provided me a home. I take care of their son when they are working. I clean the house. I do a very good job at these things. I do not earn any money, but someone in my position shouldn't. Instead I receive food and a bed. It is very generous. When my parents left me, I came here. I begged them to let me stay. I can't imagine living with the worst people ever. The Silent Order is no good. Please do not send me there. I want to stay here. I want to be good. I don't want to be evil. I want to be around good people. These are good people. They help me be good people too."

The Patrician is taken aback. He's never heard a plea like this. "Do you know why your parents left?"

Mother continues to translate, "My parents leave because it is hard to live with someone like me—someone of Silent Order. People hate them because of me. My life makes theirs too hard. They were kind and leave while I was away. They leave in middle of day. No hurtful goodbyes. It must have been hard for them." Ari is laying it on thick with her small vocabulary and almost broken English. Mother embellishes as she sees fit. Everyone is on the same page now. This is the lie we are going to tell.

"If you caused your own parents so much grief, why would you put that upon another family?" He isn't convinced yet.

Father enters the conversation before Ari has a chance to continue. "She's actually exaggerating a little bit in order to try and protect us from her shame. She didn't know what to do when she found out her parents were gone. She came here to ask, knowing that we were more knowledgeable than she. She did ask if she could stay here, but it was innocent. She has never been to see the Silent Order and is terrified of the influence they would have on her. We were actually relieved that she wanted to stay, because she's a great help with our son and keeping the house clean. We both work from home, so we can keep an eye on her and snuff out any deviant behavior. We don't experience any of the social stigma that her parents did because she is not our daughter. Everyone knows that this is an extremely cost-effective way for us to have in-home care. If she tried to charge us money, we would send her on her way immediately; but she has never done that. A bed and food is easy for us to provide and the return we get is immense. Now, I'm not sure what the legal code says, but we were planning on making a trip to Suvault next week to find out what could be done." Father had planned nothing of the sort, but it was exactly what needed to be said. "But since you're here now, maybe you can tell us: can we keep her working for us in this capacity?"

"I have never personally seen a family take in someone from the Silent Order, but there is nothing that specifically bars it from happening, and I've heard of it happening once or twice. Your situation is unique and does seem fitting for someone like her. I don't believe her account of things, but yours seems to line up. The Silent Order are known to be liars and thieves. You will need to be careful with her around. Keep your precious things locked up.

"Now, understanding the benefit you receive from her, I could allow her to stay; but I must be absolutely clear about a few things. First, if she commits any crimes while under your care, you will be held responsible insomuch as it would have been preventable by you. Next, she is not allowed to move to a new home unless she is remitted to the care of the Silent Order. Furthermore, you will not be allowed to abandon her. We understand why parents do this, and we give them some leniency considering the difficulties they are presented with; but since you are taking her on of your own volition, there will be no grace. If things become too difficult you can always contact us, and we will help remove her. Finally, I can only approve this for as long as your son is under the age of eighteen, or until he progresses to university…whichever comes first. After that, her utility will be spent and she should return to the Silent Order."

"That seems very reasonable." Father's face lights up with relief as he shakes the Patrician's hand. "Thank you for understanding our situation. We will keep a close eye on her. She's an awful little sevish sometimes, but it's really hard to find such cheap labor!" He turns to Mother, "Don't translate that last part. We don't want her getting upset."

It bothers me how quickly Father's face and tongue can become treacherous, *sevish* being the strongest derogatory term for someone of the Silent Order. He is a good actor, but my stomach is churning.

The Patrician lets out a loud laugh. "You will make a good home for her. She's very deserving of the way you treat her."

After extending a few more pleasantries with Father, the Patrician leaves. No one says anything for five minutes, wanting to be certain that he is gone. The collective sigh of relief almost moves more wind than Ari and I had less than an hour prior.

"So, did you make breakfast?" Ari decides this is the best way to break the silence. "I know we were a couple minutes late, but I didn't think you would refrain from feeding us."

This is our life: in the absence of others we speak freely; everything else that is said—all the lies we tell in our charade—we ignore.

CHAPTER 9
THE SILENT ORDER

RE: URGENT - Jameson/Hall Maidservant

Landen and Rhome have left the SO girl to fend for herself. We are still working on tracking them down. In the meantime, I sent one of my men to the Jameson/Hall home to inquire about the girl since we had a log showing they visited the house recently. Lo and behold, they were harboring her. My man reports that the family seemed to be caught off guard, but quickly covered their tracks. They requested to keep the girl so she could continue helping them. They even suggested they were going to inquire about their situation in Suvault the following week. It is convenient for them that there is no means to evaluate the veracity of that claim. In the end, my man gave them permission to keep the girl on until their son turned 18. I'm following your lead, trying to give them enough rope to hang themselves.

~ Garrison

RE: RE: URGENT - Jameson/Hall Maidservant

Find Landen and Rhome immediately! This could be the break we need.

Good job staying hands-off. They are likely breathing easy, thinking they're in the clear. In the same theme as you were suggesting, the SO girl is likely to be the *lynchpin* of this whole operation.

You have my permission to use whatever resources you deem necessary. I know you are not one for excess. Do your work and do it quickly, but remain unseen until the time is right.

~ Ward

As we sit for breakfast the tension of the morning subsides. We speak openly, enjoying each other's company, and revisiting the details of the morning.

"Ari," Father says, "I know we have discussed this before; but I cannot just let it be. The awful things we say are only meant to hide what we are doing here. I would like to formally apologize for the words I used and the indifference I showed to you."

"I started the lie. You only played your part. If anything, I made you say those words and act that way. Obviously, I'm in control of everything here and can force you to do reprehensible things. It's part of my evil nature. I *am* the worst of humanity, after all." Her mischievous grin matches everything she says.

"Well," Mother says, easing up a little, "I hope that you intend to be one of the *good* evil overlords—if that is your ultimate aim—and not one of the bad ones."

Father, having been the main perpetrator of the offense, can't quite let it go yet. "Thank you for your kindness and understanding. And again, I am sorry. It shouldn't have to be that way. But on a related note, I thought we should talk about the Silent Order. Presumably we bought ourselves eleven years to have you here with us, but that doesn't mean they won't change their minds. You may have to live with the Order at some point. I'd like you to tell us what you know about them."

Ari's forehead wrinkles as she thinks. "I don't believe they are evil."

"Why not?" Father prods.

"I'm not evil. I mean, I know that I break the law, and we even just lied to a Patrician; but the only reason I did that was because I believe the laws to be unjust. I don't believe that the three of you are evil, yet you committed the same crimes on my behalf. You think highly of me, at least enough to commit a crime. And if I am not evil, it suggests to me that not all children who are born deaf are, by nature, evil. I am only a single case study." Ari flashes a smile at Mother, knowing they recently discussed sample sizes in scientific research. "But I create a very large hole in the narrative that is taught about the Silent Order."

"Excellent," Father says, finding pleasure in her logic, "what else do you know?"

"Saree began the Silent Order, and she was the wisest person to have ever lived on Merced—so the story goes. If she held such wisdom, would she not have known the alleged corruption of those born deaf?"

"Why do you say *alleged* corruption?"

"Because the people that followed Saree didn't do so to destroy anything. She was a healer! The deaf came for help, to be accepted, and to live among a community that wouldn't be bothered by their lack of speech. The Patricians are the ones who said August Children are the best of humanity and the Silent Order are the worst. It's never been proven. The Patricians are the only ones that have a record of the Silent Order attacking them. It isn't corroborated in any other texts."

"To be fair," Father hedges, "there are a lot of texts that cover The Uprising."

"And I have read every single one of them! There isn't a single text that doesn't reiterate the account of the Patricians on the matter!"

"That's a lot of reading, Ari," Mother interjects. "We didn't assign that to you. What inspired you to take on so much?"

"I wanted to understand why I was universally hated by everyone except the three of you." Ari closes her eyes for a long second and then continues, "It's the reason I taught myself to read in the first place: to be able to understand why I was reviled by so many."

Mother and Father are shocked into silence. It's easy to forget how perceptive Ari was at such a young age and how driven she is to meet her ends.

Tentatively, Father continues, "And what did you discover?"

"Nothing!" Ari spits out with her hands. "There is no reason for people to treat me this way. There is no valid excuse." Her pace quickens. "I am not responsible for The Uprising, whatever that was. I am not the worst of humanity. I am not devoid of love and compassion. I do not deserve the maltreatment I receive." A few tears roll down her cheeks.

"For the record," Father speaks cautiously, "we are in complete agreement with you. But thank you for sharing. It's wonderful to hear that you have come to this conclusion of your own accord."

The tension in Ari's shoulders is visibly reduced. The release continues through her whole body until she continues, casually, with her breakfast as if nothing had happened at all.

"I am glad you took the initiative to discover these things," Father continues. "I hope our presence in your life has only reaffirmed what you know. Now, understanding that our situation may not last forever, how do you feel about the possibility of living with the Silent Order some day?"

"It would be fine," Air shrugs. "It's not what I want, but I'm certain they would receive me well. I would guess that they have ways of teaching the young—because keeping children from being educated is barbaric—but I don't think I would be able to learn the things I need to know. That's part of the reason I choose to stay here. Obviously, you have become my family and I am forever indebted to you; but I have ulterior motives."

"What is it that you want to do?" Mother says, eyes full of curiosity.

"I want to rewrite history," Ari says matter-of-factly. "I want to be everything the Patricians fear."

"You want to...start a war?" Father clarifies.

"No, I want to expose their lies. They say they are afraid of a war. I don't believe they are. They have the manpower to suppress any uprising that could possibly happen. It would only solidify their hegemony. What they truly fear is someone exposing their lies, causing the people of Merced to lose faith in the almighty Patricians. I want to rewrite *their* history; tell the story that actually happened. When everyone has the same exact account—word for word—of The Uprising and it only comes from one source, it can't possibly be complete."

"That would be quite the feat," Father postures. "How do you think this pursuit will affect the family around you?"

Ari glances over at me with a devilish smile; we've been waiting for this moment for quite some time. It's my turn to share what we know. "We are fairly certain you and Mother want the same exact thing; you just stopped working on it because of us. You wanted to protect us, but there's a paradox there: either you protect us by lying about your ultimate aims, which *might* keep us safe in the short term, or you pursue the course that rewrites history—which is dangerous now—but would *actually* protect us in the long run. We decided that you must have been working on this for years before our arrival. We've noticed how comfortable you are with completing work at a startling pace and turning it in at a later time. It is a refined process, and it doesn't cause you any anxiety or stress. It's obviously something you've practiced. Why are you so practiced at deception? This much is clear: you've taken in two children who you aren't allowed to have; you believe the Patricians are the enemy; and you're far too intelligent to not make any attempt at changing the injustices you see." I give a broad smile with a twinkle in my eye. "We've just been waiting for you to tell us about it."

Mother and Father are taken aback. They must have thought they kept their secret better. It is supremely satisfying to "out" this secret they have been keeping.

"Interesting hypothesis," Mother says slowly; she's processing as she speaks. "If you thought this was paramount in our lives and you wanted to be a part of it, why didn't you just bring it up and ask us about it when you first thought of it?"

"We're both too young to do anything," Ari says. "We have a lot to learn, and we have been focused on that. Eli is still just a little kid to everyone. And I'm...well...people don't exactly want me around. We figured we would bring it up when we got older; but in the meantime, if there was opportunity, we would expose your deception!" She can't contain her laughter as she points her accusing finger at them. We both contort our eyebrows into a full V shape and give our best snarls to show just how mock-angry we are. I am certain it would look quite fierce if we could keep ourselves from laughing.

"Since the two of you are so comfortable waiting for years to find out about all of this, I will neither confirm nor deny your accusations and make you wait a bit longer." Obviously, Father loves games. He is not content to be a bystander in this one. "I will confirm this one thing: Euny and I are the smartest people on this planet, just as you must have assumed we are. There is no August Child or Patrician—or even the entire Silent Order—that can match our mental acuity. We will be remembered in the history books as-"

"The narcissistic, bloviating buffoon who wouldn't stop talking about himself, and his lovely wife." Mother bats her eyes for a long second as she glares at Father. It's quite an impressive combination of looks. I'm fairly certain that Father would have continued rambling self-obsessed nonsense forever had Mother not cut him off. I think his actual intention was to go on long enough that Mother felt the need to stop him. He is clearly pleased with himself.

"Ok, I have more questions," Father announces with great passion. "What nefarious things do you believe we've been doing when we have, let's say, relieved ourselves of the burdens of the traditional working day?"

Whenever possible, Ari and I are forced to work things out on our own. Mother and Father never purposefully deprive us of an "opportunity" to problem solve—or at least that's what they tell us when we get into situations like this.

Ari is up first. "I think you read a lot, for starters. Earlier you told me I had done a lot of reading. You seemed to be confident about how much reading it was. I think you've read every one of those texts as well."

"Maybe I just like to read," Father says innocently. "I could be reading right now and you would never know!" He starts moving his eyes back and forth ever so slightly in order to give the impression that he has something he is reading on his display. After a moment, he stops. "Ok, you're right! I read all those texts. What else?"

My turn. "I think you've been in contact with the Silent Order. That's how you met Ari, isn't it? They knew her family had kept her and they were concerned for her."

Mother smiles. "It's true. I was trying to check up on her. Never in my wildest dreams did I imagine she would ask us to teach her. Our meeting in the market was the only thing that was planned."

"Tell me more about the Silent Order!" Ari blurts out, eschewing our tradition of continued problem solving. This is the only firsthand knowledge Ari has ever had access to about the Order. She is captivated.

Mother and Father understand immediately. A flash of embarrassment crosses their faces as they realize they have unintentionally kept information from Ari that she desperately desires.

"They are a kind people, Ari," Mother assures. "They would make a great home for you someday if you ever choose to live with them. You know they are an oppressed people, but they are generally left to themselves in their own village."

"How do they teach the children?" Ari interjects. "They must have a way around the law, right?"

Mother continues, "They call it the Oral Tradition; and no, the irony is not lost on them. It actually helps hide the truth in plain sight. They pass stories down to the youth as they go through their days. It just so happens that the stories they tell young children are filled with mathematics and science. As they get older the stories require advanced problem-solving skills. They have their own history of events, but it isn't written anywhere. They have another perspective on The Uprising. I am certain they will tell you the story someday. Whether you live there or not, we will be certain that you get to visit them at some point. We would have told you about all of this sooner; but you were very intent on staying with us, and we were very intent on having you. Had we known your passion and desire on the subject we would have brought it up much sooner. I'm so sorry; we didn't mean to keep it from you."

Ari is oblivious to the rest of the world around her, solely focused on Mother's words. "I am going to save my people," she vows.

"Then we have our work cut out for us, don't we?" Father looks at all of us. He won't let this be a solo event.

"How do we start?" Ari's eyes flit back and forth between Mother and Father.

"We need to learn everything we can," Father says. "Honestly, continue your education. Become the best you can possibly be. Continue to read voraciously. The answers will come in time. Had we all the answers right now it would be too dangerous to do anything, with both of you being so young. Things won't change overnight. Neither will we."

I always knew we would be heading this direction eventually. Ari and I talk about it during the mornings in our hideout sometimes. It feels strange to share it with Mother and Father. And to have it be a real—even though it will be years before we actually do anything—is something wholly new. But then it also feels exactly the same as before. We aren't going to be doing anything differently. We will study the same every day. We will practice as hard as ever. Everything just has a clearly defined purpose now. It feels good to have a purpose. It's also terrifying. How do you defeat the ruling class that controls information and has infinitely more resources than you?

Mother sees the distress on my face. "We must live our lives. We know our end pursuit, but that cannot consume our every day. I am overjoyed to have this little family. We will eat together and study together and share our lives together. We don't have a plan, and we have no idea what a plan will look like." She looks directly at me. "It would be quite distressing if we focused solely on our end goal. It is our *end* goal. We have much work to do before we get there, and a lot of time needs to pass. Let's settle into our routine and live for a while."

She's right. After a minute of silence, it's clear that nothing more needs to be said.

"Could you tell me more about the Silent Order?" Ari says quietly. She is no longer asking about details that would serve our pursuits; she is asking for herself.

"Oh, of course," Mother says soothingly, understanding the slight shift of the topic perfectly. "They are wise, Ari. They hold the wisdom of Saree with great honor. You may read that they desecrate the name of Saree; this is a bold lie. They carry on her traditions and are committed to restoring the narrative of the Silent Order to its origin. None of them are ashamed to have the name of SO. They wear it as a badge of honor."

"Some families still travel to be a part of the Silent Order," Father adds; "they cannot stand to be away from their children, nor can they stand seeing the oppression their children face. The Order is a safe community. They keep to themselves, and no one bothers them. They have never once turned away a family that wanted to join them, nor do they require vows of silence, though they do encourage everyone—both hearing and deaf—to learn sign language so they can communicate with everyone. But this isn't typically a problem since these families desperately want to communicate with their children and are often grateful to have people that can help teach them."

"The children," Ari says hesitantly, "are they...like me?"

"Are you asking if there are other little geniuses running about? Or if they use their power for evil to control their families to make them say the worst things imaginable?" Father jests, attempting to help Ari feel more comfortable about her questions.

"I remember the day I was born," Ari confesses. "I learned to sign faster than my mother. I taught myself how to read and write on my own before I was four years old. I had to practice drawing letters in the dirt so my parents wouldn't find out. I am not of August, but if Eli and I learn something new at the same time I learn it just as fast as he does."

"Almost as fast," I quip.

Ari glares at me. "*Just* as fast," she says slowly and resolutely.

I nod in agreement.

"Is everyone in the Silent Order like me?"

My parents know Ari is smart, but they had never considered asking when she became self-aware. To be fair, neither had I; but I've known since this morning. The stunned look on Mother and Father's faces must make Ari feel uncomfortable. She is squirming in her seat, her eyes darting from one to the next and then to the floor.

Mother quickly interrupts the silence. "I have never met anyone—Silent Order, August child or otherwise—that is quite like you. We have never had the opportunity to ask anyone in the Silent Order about their early years, but I can tell you this: never have I known someone that has been so committed to learning as you are." Mother looks over at Father who shakes his head vigorously to indicate he'd never met anyone like that as well. "You are unique," she continues, "special."

"Strange!" Father snorts.

Mother's hand swiftly finds the back of Father's head.

"And wonderful!" He continues with a grimace. "I was going to say, 'and wonderful.' We're all a bit strange, aren't we? It's one of my favorite things about you all."

Ari cracks a smile. Father is good at breaking tension.

"I don't know if others have had the same experience you did. You will have to ask them yourself someday. But I do know that you are one of a kind, my Ari dear. No one I have ever known is quite like you."

CHAPTER 10
UPGRADES

RE: The SO girl has returned to Evanwood

Jameson and Hall have returned the SO girl to her people. I confirmed this with the Order myself. I believe they have another girl living with them, one who's not SO. There is no law requiring families to disclose who lives in their homes, so I am unaware of her name as of yet. I sent one of my men to spy from a distance. The girl appears to be close to the same age as the boy. It seems likely they have an existing relationship; maybe she is the reason he is so well socialized despite living in a vacuum.

Landen and Rhome have proven to be difficult to find. Without any further leads I fear our investigation is coming to an end, and I may be forced to conclude—just like you said—that these are the dumbest smart people I have ever encountered.

I would still like to recommend the boy for grooming into becoming a Patrician. His test scores are still stellar across the board. I believe he would be an excellent addition, and

I must admit—after all these years—I feel a little responsible for him.

~ Garrison

RE: RE: The SO girl has returned to Evanwood

You have done good work. Sending away the SO girl really does seem to deflate all the various theories I had going about the family. We'll leave the case open in case any leads fall our way, but I think it's reasonable to downgrade them to a threat level 1.

Feel free to continue to track the boy. If you think he would make a good addition, then I believe he would make a good addition. It's sweet of you to care for him. He's been your charge since birth, really. Getting him away from his parents is very much in his best interest. Still, we'll likely have to wait until university. Wait it out and I'll give you whatever resources you need when the time is right.

~ Ward

"Hewn together like the waters of that loch, I impressed the French queen in her beige gown. Again, she heard that a young Arthur just wanted to play the symphony as he had before, including all of the parts on the violin."

"Good, again."

"Hewn together like the waters of that loch, I impressed the French quane-"

"Queen."

"Queen."

"Good, again."

"Hewn together like the waters of that loch, I impressed the French queen in her beige gown. Again, she heard that a young Arthur just wanted to play the symphony as he had before, including all of the parts on the violin."

Our morning routine has changed, but only slightly. Now, while we practice our shifting forms as we wait for our charges to build back up, Ari also practices her speaking form. We are months past good enough, but she wants perfection. Any mistakes she makes now are not because she doesn't know how to say the word, but because she is practicing slight variations of a particular sound, using my correction to identify the small differences between good enough and perfect. And, since Ari has never found "good enough" to actually be good enough, I am to correct her on every nuance so she has an immediate comparison to work against.

At my request, Father brought home the audio mods for Ari nearly two years ago. It feels like yesterday. "They were easy enough to come by," he had said. "They are typically injected into ears and amplify sound so those with hearing loss can...well...hear better. They are essentially…isn't it 'hearing aids' that you've described, Eli? Well, anyhow, they don't require batteries or anything. They draw all the power they need from your body. Once injected, they can't be seen. Our CI already works together with all our senses, giving us the ability to record video and audio based on what we see and hear. For Ari, no sound is ever recorded, since her auditory nerves are damaged beyond repair. Medical technology on Merced is quite advanced, so it's possible her nerves could be fixed with further study; but no one is ever interested in devoting their time and effort to help the Silent Order. As we all know, it's not exactly an approved field of study. But now I'm rambling.

"Well, like I said, implants are easy enough to come by. What's more expensive is the program to operate them properly. I don't know exactly what you intend to do with them, but the two of you seem like you have some brainy idea and I just can't bring myself to stop you. But you understand these just won't work for Ari, right? I'm sorry, dear, but no matter how loud you turn these up, you won't be able to hear? Other than that…I'm sure you'll surprise me with what you're able to cook up."

Hearing was never the goal. First, we wrote a program that converts speech to text. Most people hide the display of their CI unless they are using it, since it blocks a fair amount of vision; but Ari had the idea to make the display transparent while pertinent data is opaque.

"Remember that time you ran into that tree?" Ari laughed out. "I programmed my first transparent display after that. I knew you liked to have your display up to see your heart rate. I didn't ever want to be dumb like you and run into a tree because I couldn't see past my CI."

We created a program for Ari that always runs in the background. Every word spoken aloud is converted into text and displayed a little below her main line of vision. To the right and left of the text a maximum of three arrows light up, indicating the direction and proximity of the speaker. It wasn't perfect at first, but we continued to refine it for over a year. Every day, we spent hours. That first month must have been at least ten hours a day working out all the kinks and testing incessantly. The work has slowed, though. Now it's only minor errors once or twice a week. It's already functional, but we won't stop until there aren't any more errors.

This entire project is one of the coolest things I've ever worked on in either of my lives. Rudimentary sound detection might have been my favorite part. We added it only a few weeks in. "Of course you can design what the sounds look like," Ari had said, "You were an artist, weren't you?" I picked my favorite onomatopoeias and surrounded them with jagged clouds that emblazon each "POW!" and "BANG!". "It's like a fight scene in a comic book," I had explained. "I know that no one here even knows what a comic book is, but it's something that I loved when I was young and I thought you might appreciate the style for this application." She loved it.

We associated each sound with a specific word that appears directly below the main text line. Each sound is also accompanied by the set of arrows to the left and right. A special piece of programming I was proud of changes the size of the sound-word based on loudness; the higher the decibel, the larger the word. Excessively loud sounds flash once, at their onset, in the middle of her vision. The idea is that she should be startled by large noises, just like everyone else. This is how you appear to fit in.

The next program we created was an audio wave analyzer. As people speak, the audio waves are modeled directly above each word. When Ari speaks, it shows her own audio waves and compares them to waves of the same word numerous other people have spoken. While there is a lot of variation in waves based on the timbre of someone's voice and how they say a word, it is helpful for Ari to see where major differences are, especially when comparing several waves of the same word. Then, she practices and alters her pronunciation and the shape of her mouth to try and match the other waves more closely.

After all the programming was done we started using a phonetic pangram—a sentence that includes every phonetic sound in the English language. "The quick brown fox jumped over the lazy dog" is the most commonly used pangram I have ever heard, using each letter of the alphabet at least once. Phonetic pangrams are a bit trickier. I only remember parts of one I heard on Earth. We worked to fill in the missing pieces. It's probably longer than it needs to be, but it does the trick. We made dozens of shorter phrases that emphasize specific sounds she has trouble with. Sometimes I choose words that have no meaning to her, but she learns to pronounce them nonetheless.

"It's a style, syllable, sassafras, salutation. Temple, temporal, thimble, tumble, Thumbelina. Plate, inflate, cellulite, flight, plight."

Three or four phrases put together properly and Ari returns to the main event: "Hewn together like the waters of that loch, I impressed the French queen in her beige gown. Again, she heard that a young Arthur just wanted to play the symphony as he had before, including all of the parts on the violin."

Purpose. Everything needs a purpose. Ari wants the ability to walk through a crowd…unnoticed. The conversation with Mother and Father happened three years ago:

"I need a new identity: one that won't be stopped every time a Patrician sees me...one that won't be sneered at by people passing by."

"Ari, dear," Mother said sympathetically, "it's not a simple task. You would have to be able to pass yourself off in every way as someone who is not deaf. I know you can read lips, but as soon as you speak people would know. No new identity would fix that. Please understand, we see you as perfect just the way you are, with no need for change; but if you want something else, you will have to find a way for every part of you to blend in."

"So, if I can pass myself off as someone who is not deaf, you'll help me get a new identity?" She wasn't deterred in the least.

"When you're fifteen," Father interjected, "we will evaluate the situation and see. It's dangerous, and I just don't feel comfortable doing it until you're at least fifteen."

"Fine with me." Her grin spanned her whole face. "It's not important to have right now. I just need it by the time we make a plan. I don't want to be left out of anything because of my identity."

Today is the day. Ari is turning fifteen. She has kept up her end of the deal. In a short while we will find out if Mother and Father have been able to hold up their end.

We are done waiting; it has been long enough. We can practice shifting one last time and then head home. For the last year we have been practicing our solo skills first thing in the morning and then in tandem at the end of our time to see what, if anything, we can create. Our individual efforts surpassed Father's long ago, though we are still ages away from being able to walk on the wind, if it's even possible.

"It's possible!" Ari says, breaking my concentration.

"What? I didn't say anything."

"I know that look on your face where you start to reminisce about everything and then you eventually end up in the same place, wondering if it's possible to walk on the wind. I know you, Eli...I know everything about you," she grins maniacally. "But enough of that. It's time."

Ari raises her hands above her head and waves them in a circle. The motion makes her whole body sway, though her feet remain planted—rooted against the gale force wind that's to come. It's an elegant dance of sorts. Don't get distracted again. Can't get distracted again. I don't know what I could say to explain myself this time. Ari's job today is to create and maintain the wind for as long as she can. Steady, consistent, controlled, it circles the walls of our fort. My job is exactly the opposite; I need to expel as much energy as I can as quickly as I can. I stand next to Ari, my arms raised in the same way hers are. With my muscles tensed, as though I am manipulating a great weight, I arch my back and move in the opposite direction of Ari. While she slowly builds up and maintains the swirling force over a period of ten seconds, I use everything I have in less than two. As I move the wind, the force I create collides with Ari's, moving the opposite direction, consuming all of Ari's wind in the process. It grows as it collects more and more until it has circled the room and there is nothing more to gather. For a brief second our clothing settles on our bodies as the wind stops swirling. Then, with sharp, precise movements, we throw our arms in front of us. Our combined force is thrust directly ahead of us and ricochets off the wall, nearly knocking us over. Were we not prepared it would have put us on our backs.

Progress has been slow over the years, but it is still progress. Every day we switch positions. We each want to be capable of creating in both positions, and we also find that a thorough understanding of what the other is doing helps us pair our abilities together. Today is the best we have ever done. We are both eager with anticipation; I think our emotional state alters our abilities in some ways. No matter the cause, we both feel all the more energized for the rest of our day after such a resounding success. We suit up and are home within minutes.

"Happy birthday!" Mother and Father shout as we enter the back door.

Ari laughs out loud and turns to me. "This is your doing, isn't it?"

"I don't think Eli had anything to do with you being born so many years ago," Father says, "nor did he ask us to tell you happy birthday." He looks back and forth between the two of us to find out exactly where the fun is so he can be a part of it too.

Ari laughs again. "Every time someone says happy birthday..." the giggling is nearly uncontrollable and infectious, "(even when I say it!) confetti and fireworks cover my entire display!"

"Maybe—just maybe—last week, when we were doing an update on the language program, I added a few lines of code that create confetti and fireworks every time someone tells you happy birthday. Actually, it doesn't matter who they say it to. But it only happens on your birthday." It is harmless fun. Now that she knows it's there, she can go in any time she wants and change it.

"Well, since the festivities are in full swing, let's continue with a present." Mother shares her display with all of us. Front and center are identification documents. "Your new identity is Arin Salven Gentry. It makes it so we can still call you Ari without anyone being the wiser. These documents are a forgery, as you might have guessed, but they are the best forgery we could muster. Anyone you show them to should be satisfied. If, for some reason, they decide to check your documents against the database we have written in a...Eli, what did you call it?"

"A Trojan horse!"

"Right, we've written in a Trugcian horse." Mother pronounced it wrong the very first time I told her about it. We all made fun of her and now she refuses to say it properly out of blissful spite. "The Teragian horse is inside your documentation and when it gets to the database it automatically sends back a positive match. It also leaves a record in the database as if it had always existed there. It then removes itself after thirty minutes so it doesn't raise any red flags for a database analyst. There are definitely things that could go wrong, but since you've kept up your end of the deal we had to keep up ours, and no one should be able to identify you as a member of the Silent Order. In the end, it's in your best interest to tread carefully. If you were taken into custody for some reason, I'm sure you would be found out. I guess I'm just trying to tell you to be safe.

"These documents also show that Isaac and I are your caretakers. We sent documents to Suvault a week ago stating that Arielle Linivette SO was no longer needed and would be sent to live with the Silent Order. The Order was kind enough to confirm your arrival. They don't know much about you, and we have shared as little as possible. They know we have common goals and while our communication is secure, it is understood that secrets are best kept by not sharing them."

"This is perfect; thank you so much!" Ari says with impeccable tone and inflection. Typically, inside our home, she signs and vocalizes at the same time. At this moment, her hands are still and she appears as an ordinary girl without any impairments. Yes, let's let everyone believe she is ordinary; her documentation is not the only Trojan horse.

"Now, I know we haven't known each other for all that long," Ari begins skeptically, "but I'm fifteen, not thirteen."

Taking a second look at the documents I see that they do, in fact, state that she is thirteen years old.

"Euny and I were concerned about making you the same age as Arielle," Father explains. "It might look strange and cause someone to look into it further. So, we changed your age. I hope it doesn't bother you too much."

"Ari," I say as I place my hand on her shoulder and hang my head low, "I'm sorry, but in the past, I respected you because of your age and wisdom. Being four years my elder held some weight. Unfortunately, I can no longer keep your company as I have come to find out that you are only two years my elder. It's just not the same. I hope you can understand."

She smiles back at me. "A fifteen-year-old Ari would have had the wisdom and compassion to hear you, understand your concerns, and give you the space you needed. Unfortunately, thirteen-year-old Ari doesn't have quite the same handle on her emotions and is inclined towards acts of violence when provoked." With that she slaps me on the back of the head—not hard enough to cause real pain, but it does sting a little. She turns to my parents who are stifling laughs. "Thank you for this, it is perfect. There is nothing more I could have asked for from you." Then, turning back to me, she proclaims in a self-righteous tone, "And now, since it's my birthday, I want stories about Earth over breakfast."

From cat videos to social media, the three of them are obsessed with the mundane and trivial things from Earth. I close my eyes and shake my head to patronize them…I knew this was coming today. They also love my stories about cartoon characters and superheroes, and it isn't just on me to tell the story; they all ask the most ridiculous questions and react in the strongest way possible to the smallest of things. We once had a two-hour conversation discussing the merits of blind mice and whether or not they would have the ability to run after a farmer's wife. And that was before I got to line about their tails being cut off. They all started yelling and screaming about how inhumane it was. When I finally reached the end and told them it was a nursery rhyme for children, Father just got up, flipped his chair over in disgust and left the room. To his credit, he stuck with the bit and did not return.

"Do you want to hear something fantastic about Earth, or something awful? Full disclosure: I've been saving something truly awful for this occasion, but it's your choice since it's your birthday."

Mother and Father scuttle into the kitchen to grab our food while Ari is pondering her choices. She remains in thoughtful repose until the food is served and everyone is seated.

"I know you like telling us sweet things about your original home, but I'm ready to hear something terrible. Please understand that we, as a family, will disown you if at least one of us doesn't pop a blood vessel."

"Fear not. I'm not joking about saving this one. I've been itching to tell you for years, but I wanted to save it for a special occasion; and that is today."

"Let us begin with the stories of old." Father announces me as if I were a character in one of Shakespeare's plays. He loves the pageantry. There was an August Child once that was an Old English professor on Earth. He travelled around Merced acting out small snippets of plays for crowds. Evidently, there was some heavy editing involved. Mother and Father had heard most of Romeo and Juliet before. So, when they asked me to retell the story, I didn't hold back any details. When I got to the end, it didn't go over well.

"Let this day commemorate what ought not be repeated in history henceforth, heretofore, and as such." Father also works very hard to make sure what he says is complete nonsense.

Deep breath...here we go. "Let's say you wanted to measure something; how would you do it?" I want to start them off easy.

"When I want to measure things, I just measure them." Mother says with a mouth half full of food. They seriously devolve into Neanderthals whenever we do this.

"Yes, but what system would you use?"

"I would use the system of measurement!" Father exclaims. "Did I get it right?" It is typical of Father to try and win, even though it isn't a competition. I would say that they don't make any effort in their responses, but they actually do make severe efforts to avoid anything resembling a correct answer.

"I'm afraid that is not correct; and again, I must let you know, I take away points every time you ask if you got something right."

Father brings his body low to the table, his eyes bulging a little as he stares me down. "So how many points do I have now?"

"Moving on."

Father just shrugs me off and goes back to his food as I continue. "We have a very nice system of measurement here on Merced. How many meters are in a kilometer?"

"Obviously 1000," Ari chimes in. "Did you seriously save grade school questions for my birthday?"

"We're getting there, be patient. How many centimeters in a meter?"

"100, and there's ten millimeters in a centimeter," Mother says with irritation in her voice. "Need we go further?"

"What if I asked you how many milliliters were in a liter."

"This had better get good fast," Air complains. "So far this is not the birthday surprise you promised it would be. The answer is 1000, but you should know that already because we covered it with your quiz on meters. It's all the same anyway. Why are you asking us stupid questions? Are *you* stupid."

"You know," Father speaks with wonderment in his voice, "I think he just might be."

Mother nods in agreement while chewing a full mouth of food.

"I assure you that I am not stupid, but what I'm about to divulge will be. Let me tell you about where I come from. Most of Earth uses this very same measurement system that we have been discussing, but my home—"

"The United States! Did I get it right?"

I roll my eyes at Father and give a long sigh. "Now, where I'm from, we had a different system. It was called the Standard system."

"Why would you call it the Standard system if it clearly isn't standard?" Mother says indignantly. "You could call it the Less Standard system, or the Alternative system; but certainly not Standard. If *most* of Earth uses one system, then another system is not standard. Do they understand the meaning of words in your home land?"

"That is precisely the problem, and it's just the beginning. Let's consider distance, for starters. The closest relative we have to the kilometer is the mile. The mile is broken up into feet. Would anyone like to venture a guess as to how many feet are in a mile?"

"1000. Okay, so they have different names for measurement, big deal. When does this get good?" Ari's patience is wearing thin.

"No, not 1000." They all stop eating and look up at me. Their collective interest is piqued. Time to drop the hammer. "There are 5,280 feet in a mile."

"Why?" Father gasps. "Why would someone do that? What is that? Why? What do you mean 5,280? How would that make any sense at all?"

"Not done yet." They all pause, shock coursing through their eyes. They truly thought I was done already. "A foot is approximately the size of a human foot. It was standardized some time ago. I just want you to have some frame of reference."

"Every measurement system has to start somewhere," Mother grants. "The foot is fine, but is there nothing between a foot and a mile? Meters are a much better unit of measure."

"Euny's right," Father agrees, "you should add meters to your so called Standard system."

"We don't have meters, but we do have a yard. A yard is three feet."

"This is awful," Ari says with disgust. "I approve! Tell me more awful things about Earth." If I didn't know better I'd say that she is currently transfixed by a train wreck. No trains on Merced, so that must not be the case.

"Why didn't you go from miles to yards and then to feet?" Mother questions. "Why skip yards?" There it is; the order is solidified: Father, Ari, Mother. That order will follow through the rest of story time. One time Father complained about his "turn" being skipped and since then they always choose to speak in order. Once the rotation is locked in, they will not deviate. They will fume and fume until it is their turn, but they *always* follow the order.

"No one knows how many yards are in a mile. I mean, we could easily figure it out; but no one does it. You learn how many feet are in a mile, but never how many yards are in a mile."

"That's stupid."

"Yes, Father…yes, it is. Now let's continue: smaller than a foot is the inch. Would anyone like to venture a guess as to how many inches are in a foot?" I address all of them, but I am fully aware it's Ari's turn.

"It should be ten."

"Yes, you are correct!"

"That's normal. I thought this wasn't something that was going to be normal." Mother feigns disappointment. This is not an uncommon role for her.

"You misunderstand; she is correct that it *should* be ten, but it's not actually ten. It's twelve."

"Why would you do that? Eli, seriously, why? What is wrong with you? Did we not love you enough as a child? Was I a bad father? Did someone hurt you? Who hurt you, Eli?" He pauses for dramatic effect. "What if I want to know how many inches are in a mile? Are you expecting me to multiply twelve by 5,280? That's ludicrous!"

"Just wait, there's more."

At this moment, none of them are exactly sure what to do. Usually I only give them one piece of information to freak out about. This has them truly disturbed. They stare with wide eyes in anticipation.

"An inch is the smallest standard unit of measure. After that we have fractions of an inch."

"No centi-inches?" Air says blandly. "Wouldn't you want them in tenths? Those are fractions. Great fractions. Aren't those the fractions you're going to use? Or do you have some special new name for them?"

"Unfortunately, those are not the fractions I'm going to use; I'm sorry. It's nothing that simple. Inches are, at first, divided up into 16th's."

"Get out!" Mother forcefully points towards the back door. "I know I gave birth to you, but some things are unforgivable!"

"Does it make you feel any better that after sixteenths there are times when you have to break them up into 32nd's and 64th's? For accuracy, of course."

Father's voice is slow, methodical, cutting...every syllable pronounced with exact precision through clenched teeth. "How dare you treat your mother that way! You are not to speak those filthy words in here ever again! 64th's…" he spits towards the ground.

"Did I forget to mention that volume does not follow the same pattern?"

"Eli," Ari whispers, "you've told us some heinous things about Earth before, but this is by far the most egregious thing I have ever heard." She wipes the imaginary sweat from her brow, showing how exhausting it is to learn these things. "You should stop before someone gets hurt."

Time to rip the Band-Aid off. "A gallon is a fair bit bigger than a liter. There are four quarts in a gallon and two pints in a quart, two cups in a pint, and eight fluid ounces in a cup. Please note that fluid ounces are not the same as ounces, which are a measure of weight. There are sixteen ounces in a pound–"

"What is your problem?" Mother screams, "And why do you keep on insisting that sixteen is a reasonable divisor?"

"If it makes you feel any better, there are 2000 pounds in a ton."

"You knew that wouldn't make your mother feel better!" Father accuses. "You told her that just to hurt her more!"

"Also, the abbreviation for pound is L-B."

"That can't be right because the word 'pound' doesn't contain either of those letters." Ari says, voice quivering with fear. "You must be mistaken. Explain to us right now about how you are mistaken."

"No mistake here." My head shrinks back. I am a turtle withdrawing from danger. "Did I mention that there are two tablespoons in a fluid ounce and there are three teaspoons in a tablespoon? After that we're back to fractions again. Half a teaspoon, quarter, eight–"

"Do *not* say it or I swear you are dead to me." Mother looks exhausted, on the verge of tears.

"Sixteenths."

Mother screams as her head falls into Father's lap.

"You knew what this would do to her and you went ahead with it anyway. You are a monster!" Father shouts.

"I noticed you said there were half teaspoons, but what happens if I need half a tablespoon?" Ari has already worked out the math, I am sure of it. Deep down, I think she wants to incite Mother further.

"Um, you aren't typically given the option to have half a tablespoon. You could have a teaspoon and half a teaspoon. That would make up half a tablespoon, I guess."

Mother's head raises above the table for just a moment, hand on her forehead, anger filling her voice, "Sixths? You just broke a tablespoon up into sixths in order to make a half!" It's too much for her. She faints, falling back again into Father's lap. The theatrics are impressive.

We continue on for a half hour, long past finishing our food. Father offers that Ari could be their only child instead of me. Ari declines since she doesn't want to have any official association with me, even if I am kicked out of the family. Having the same parents would be too much. Mother faints at least four more times, though she manages to come out of it just enough to say something every time it is her turn. It is one of the most entertaining Earth sessions we have ever had.

As Ari, Mother and I clear the dishes from breakfast, Father sneaks off into another room. He emerges with fervor in his step and presents Ari with a small gray box. It sits in the palm of his hand. "Happy birthday," he says shyly.

Ari cracks a smile as the confetti fills her vision once again. I'm certain Father said it intentionally in order to make the moment a little more festive. "This is intended for you and Eli; but it's your birthday, so you get to open it."

My interest is piqued. Here's to platitudes about great things and small packages. Ari takes the box and carefully removes the top. Whatever is inside isn't heavy; the entire box lifts from the suction as Ari pulls up on the lid. Once open we see four electronic chips. More audio mods?

Before we mutter a word Father answers all our questions. "They are camera mods. They work in conjunction with your CI, just like Ari's audio mods. They are typically used to enhance failing eyesight, but I believe they can also be placed just under the skin on the outside rim of your ear. Now you can actually have eyes in the back of your heads, or I guess in the back of your ears."

Before Father finishes explaining, Ari moves to a chair directly in front of me, facing away. Her dark, wavy hair hangs over the back of the chair, reaching a few inches below her shoulders. I immediately begin to braid it. Once the father of a little girl, always the father of a little girl—braids are my specialty.

We had planned on making a trip to the market today to test out Ari's new identity. She has never spoken to anyone outside of Mother, Father and I, but this is too exciting. The market will have to wait. Today is a day for modifications.

"The chips weren't terribly expensive to come by; but again, it's the programming that costs." Father's tone changes from explanatory to apologetic. "Unfortunately, I couldn't afford to purchase the program, so I'm afraid these may be useless to you," he jests.

Ari nods politely, a stupid smile stuck to her face. I can't even see it. I just know it's there. I am too busy to give Father the time of day. He could have told us we were being sacrificed to a volcano later in the day and neither of us would have cared.

"Done!"

A small braid runs down each side of Ari's head. They begin at her temples, flow over her ears, and then attach together at their ends. The two braids effectively corral the rest of her wild, twisted hair. Ari loves her curls. So do I. There is no way I am taking that away from her. It is only necessary to clear her ears. The braids do their job perfectly. Step one, complete.

Neither of us had noticed, but mother left and returned already with an injection gun. She places a chip in each of our ears, and then we are off. We don't actually go anywhere. We just plant ourselves at the table and begin to write the program.

"Happy birthday, happy birthday, happy birthday, happy birthday! I'm going to win!" I don't care that we are working on the program together. The intensity of the moment still feels like competition.

Ari hits me on the shoulder.

"You have a strong punch for a thirteen-year-old."

She turns to me and scowls for a long second and then returns to work.

While we would have preferred a feeding tube, we manage to eat the food Mother and Father place in front of us at meal times. I don't know what it is beyond sustenance. I'm sure it tastes good, but my focus is elsewhere. Fourteen hours in and we have a working program.

I close all of my other displays. What I see in front of me now is two screens. They remind me of side view mirrors on a car. I move them from the central position to the outer range of my vision. Next, I bring the opacity down to 50%. I can see through them, but I can also see what's going on behind me. It's not a high definition image—the camera *is* set behind a layer of skin—but it's clear enough. Functional, in this case, is actually good enough. I won't always want them on, but I'll leave it for several days until I get used to it.

The camera is doubly good for Ari; she can now see who is speaking behind her. She may not always be able to read their lips from the feed, but she won't need to. She already has audio converted to text. These cameras just provide more context.

For the last five minutes, as we've been customizing our new video feeds, Mother and Father have been acting out Romeo and Juliet behind us, wanting to know if our program actually works. They're signing all the lines so we can see what they're saying, yet they remain silent. They have each stabbed themselves multiple times. I would say they forgot about the poison, but I think they just wanted more dramatic dying scenes.

"Euny, I mean, Juliet! I love you; so I'm going to stab myself, because I love you." Father's body revolts as he plunges his empty hands into his stomach.

"I love you more, so I will also stab myself because my death is a metaphor for love somehow." Mother slowly presses the butt end of her closed fist against her chest, waits several seconds, and then convulses her whole body a single time.

"Why are we stabbing ourselves?"

"Because of our love. Don't you get it?"

"Of course I get it. I was asking to make sure you got it."

"Of course I got it. Don't you love me?"

"I love you so much that I will stab myself again!"

Having tested our video feeds with Mother and Father's exuberant display, both Ari and I are done for the day. She gets up and walks over to my parents.

"You are my family and I love you," she signs. "Should I also stab myself in an attempt to show the full measure of my affection?"

Father, lying on the ground and gasping for air, reaches up to hand Ari an invisible knife. "This is the only true form of affection. Use this well so we can know the depth of your love for us."

With that, Ari stabs herself in the neck with her imaginary knife. Her dying scene is even more dramatic than Mother and Father's, arms waving about wildly, nearly falling over multiple times, and finally landing on the ground between my parents. The three of them let out a collective sigh, signaling their last breaths.

I stand, walk to the pile of bodies on the floor, and turn my back to them so I can address the audience that was never there. "Ladies and gentlemen, the story has been told, that of Arielle, Juliet and her Romeo. Let this lesson, shared this season, show that true love...is about stabbing oneself with a knife and dying for no apparent reason."

Right on cue, the three of them stand up, hold hands, and give a bow. I quickly move to the side, waving my arm in their direction in order to deflect the nonexistent praise from the nonexistent crowd. They wait a full minute for the applause to die down, give one final bow, and exit stage left. The show is over.

CHAPTER 11
EXPOSED

RE: We have located Landen and Rhome

After more than ten years we finally have a credible citing. They did not want to be found. I'm headed to the Seltan plains today to deal with this in person. I will be certain this is handled correctly and will report back as soon as I have information for you.

~ Garrison

RE: RE: We have located Landen and Rhome

Excellent work. You are aware of their crimes. Proceed accordingly.

~ Ward

RE: We have taken Landen and Rhome

I recorded our interactions today. Transcript is below.

~ Garrison

"Are you Savana Rhome?"

"Yes, can I help you with something? It's not often that we have a Patrician visit our home."

"Is your husband home as well? I'd like to speak with the both of you."

"Certainly, come in. My husband is in the living room. You can have a seat in there. James, this is...I'm sorry, I missed your name."

"Garrison."

"Thank you, Mr. Garrison. What can we do for you?"

"Let me say first that neither of you are being charged with anything. I can see that concerned look on your face. This is just a checkup to gather information. So please be forthright with your answers to my questions. The information you provide is valuable and we appreciate you sharing with us. Do you both understand?"

"Yes, thank you."

"And you, Mr. Rhome?"

"Yes…"

"It came to our attention a little over ten years ago that a deaf child was abandoned: Arielle Linivette SO. We are very understanding of parents that leave children of the Silent Order. These children start off as precious babies, but we all know the monsters they turn into and parents leaving is very common. The social pressure alone is burdensome beyond belief. I assume you experienced this. We don't actively seek out parents, but when we come across them we like to find out the circumstances surrounding their departure. Would you mind sharing your story with me?"

"I told Savana from the first day we found out that we should get rid of her—ungrateful little girl never listened to a word I said!"

"She was deaf!"

"Oh, so you're defending her? Do you want to have this argument all over again?

I thought we were past this."

"I was just trying to explain that she never really knew you because she couldn't hear or speak. I wasn't trying to defend her."

"That little witch knew exactly what I was saying. I could see it in her eyes. She learned to read lips and never told us. We could have gone to jail for her crimes! And we may yet."

"Mr. Rhome, let me assure you, nothing you share with us today will incriminate you. We are well aware of how difficult it is to have a child of this nature. I sympathize with you. I just need to hear what happened. Savana, do you maybe want to start and then James, you can fill in some details as we go?"

"I don't know where to begin."

"Just tell me your story, beginning to end."

"Well, we were excited to have a baby. I mean, I know I was very excited and I think James was excited about it too. I had always wanted a little girl. The day of her birth was one of the best days of my life, or at least it felt like it at the time. We were so happy; she was so beautiful. I had concerns after a few days. She wasn't responding to any noises. Our fears were confirmed on her naming day: she was a child of the Silent Order. I couldn't bear to see her go; James and I fought for days. I knew she wasn't the little girl that I had always wanted, but she was so small and so innocent. I know now just how wrong I was about that, but at the time I couldn't fathom such a small baby being anything other than precious. In the end, we decided to keep her for a while. I brought home books in order to learn sign language and to teach Arielle. And I promise, I never intended to teach her anything more than basic communication."

"That's fine. I will say it as many times as necessary: nothing you say today will be held against you. We only want to know what happened. When parents abandon children of the Silent Order they do so for good reason. We understand that; you have nothing to fear."

"Thank you for that. As I was saying, I brought picture books home to teach Arielle how to sign. A few months in I realized she was learning faster than I was. I had always thought she was just playing with the books, but she was studying. Her hands couldn't form words as well as mine could, and she rarely signed more than a word at a time, but I would watch her with the books. She couldn't hear me, so she wouldn't notice me observing from behind. She would look at the book and then try and make the shape with her hand. I've never seen a child so young do such a thing. I couldn't believe it. Literally, I could not believe it. It's not possible for children that young to learn on their own. I decided I must be seeing things.

"As time passed she asked for more and more books. She always told me, 'Pictures, pictures, I want more pictures,' but what she wanted was an education. Sure, she would show me the brightest and prettiest pictures she could find, but I saw what she was doing when I was out of the room: she was learning. I can't believe I was so foolish. I couldn't bear to lose her though, so I decided that my eyes must be deceiving me. I knew the truth, but I couldn't fathom it. It's hard to believe something that is so improbable.

"When she was three I returned to work for a few hours a day. Arielle was self-sufficient, so we left her at home, alone. Things came to a bit of a head a year later when James came home early from work one day."

"That's right...I found her in my study. She had several books open. I don't know how, but she had learned to read. I was ready to send her away right then and there, but Savana still didn't want to. I was very mad, but I couldn't blame her; the mothering instinct is very strong. It's not just something you can shake off, even if your child *is* abhorrent. So, we fought again...for weeks. I wasn't sure we were going to make it through intact, but then the best thing happened: a couple with a new baby needed help taking care of their home and they wanted to make use of Arielle. Believe me, they needed the help; their house was disgusting. They couldn't handle anything and were desperate. We needed a place where Arielle could be during the day, and this was a perfect fit. I think cleaning and caring for babies is a fine job for anyone in the Silent Order. I was very, very pleased with the situation. Well, I was pleased at first. Things became troubling as time passed. I can't even talk about it without becoming angry. Savana, you should continue."

"Well, like James said, we were very excited to have Arielle working for another family. It solved many of the issues we were concerned about, but then I started to notice things. First, her signing form had improved, and then she had new words that I had never learned. I assumed she was just gleaning things from interacting with other people; we all change how we talk a little if we spend a lot of time with people. But then I noticed that Arielle seemingly tracked our conversations. She would never tell us anything, but she looked at us very intently when we were speaking. I think she learned to read lips. I don't know how that would happen without training of some sort, so I was very concerned. I started sharing small details with James that I would never sign to Arielle—things like what time we were going to leave for something. Just small things. Then I would tell Arielle a general time to be ready, like morning or afternoon, but she would always be ready at the exact time I had told James. As time passed she left earlier and earlier and arrived home later and later. She always said it was for her work, but I think it's because she was being educated somewhere. I don't know who would educate a girl from the Silent Order, but she must have had help."

"Do you think the family she was working for was helping her learn?"

"No, like James said, they were unimaginably disorganized. They wouldn't have had any time to think about Arielle beyond the little instructions they would give her for cleaning or taking care of the baby."

"Let me frame this differently for the two of you. Isaac Jameson is an architect. I have reviewed his work and it includes some of the most pristine designs I have ever seen. I don't think there is an architect working in Suvault that has a better grasp on how to work with trees. Eunice Hall is a biologist, though she could have been nearly anything she wanted. She received mastery scores in seven competencies on her entrance exam to university. Her work in the field was revolutionary, helping us understand what the trees need to thrive after being formed into homes and buildings. A few years before their son was born they started working from home, collaborating on projects. Not only is their work phenomenal, it is now the standard by which all projects are evaluated. We routinely use their work as examples when designing new projects. No one knew Isaac's code had any faults until he started working with Eunice; together they make something special. I have not been to their home, but their work is extremely organized and competent. Considering this information, do you think Isaac and Eunice are the type of people that would have a dysfunctional home?"

"Are you suggesting that they tricked us?"

"I'm not suggesting anything—only filling in details you may not have so I can more accurately understand your perception of the situation."

"I don't know. Savana and I only visited them once. It was chaotic. We've said it before, but they were desperate. If what you're saying is true...I don't know. Their work doesn't sound like people who are desperate."

"So, you sent your daughter to them every day, but you only ever visited them once?"

"Look—just like Savana told you—I didn't want her around at all, but it seemed better than to send her away to live with all the other vile people from Earth. At least here she would be around good people, or at least we thought they were good people."

"You must have known that things weren't right. You must have had some idea that this family wasn't forthcoming with you. A wise man would have checked in more—would have been more vigilant. I know you didn't want Arielle, but you had a responsibility to protect the people around you from her."

"I didn't want her, but Savana did. I could live with that because I love Savana. I did what I could to find a place for Arielle. I didn't want to poke holes in it or distrust other people in the process. I don't think you understand the kind of stigma we faced as parents of a…freak. We were always in danger of losing our jobs, we had no friends, our families shunned us and we were cut off from everyone we ever loved. A family offered to take a substantial portion of our burden and when we checked in to it we saw that they were in need. Maybe everything didn't quite line up, but it was the best option we had."

"I see. Thank you for sharing. What happened next? What inspired you to finally leave?"

"James and I were both working late one day, but I got off before he did. Arielle wasn't expecting me home yet. When I got to the front door I heard something. Instead of opening the door I waited and listened. It was crude and sounded wrong, but she was practicing words...she was speaking. Once I was certain of what was going on I entered the house. She stopped as soon as she saw the door move. I told her I was tired and needed to go to bed, then I waited in my room for James to get home. We made plans to leave the next day. We both resigned from our jobs and neither one of us saw her again.

"I'm sorry we didn't come forward to say something. We didn't know how understanding you would be and we were worried that we would be seen as complicit in Arielle's crimes. We were not, but we were scared and possibly a little foolish."

"So you moved to the Seltan plains—about as far away from Sova as you can get. The communities here are small in number, but cover a great distance. The extra space makes it easy to blend in—keeping you out of the spotlight. You spelled your names differently on official documents and were able to hide in plain sight. I can't say I blame you."

"It was far enough away that nobody knew us. For the first time in ages both Savana and I were able to make friends. We could work without threat of being fired. We could live our lives again, no longer held down by the burden of that girl."

"And then you promised each other not to tell anyone of your past, but one of you just couldn't help yourself, right?"

"No. Savana and I remained quiet on the matter. We've never shared with anyone."

"Savana, is that the truth?"

"James—I'm sorry—it just came out one day when I was talking with another mother. She was sharing with me about when her daughter was a baby and I shared something without even thinking about it. Then I had to explain our situation and she promised not to tell anybody. I'm so sorry. I've tried very hard not to tell anybody, but I guess it's not such a big deal. It all worked out just fine."

"It's true that she did promise not to tell anyone, but she broke that promise. You see, your friend decided it was best to adhere to the rule of law. She contacted us and that's how we are here with you today."

"Savana, it's fine. I don't blame you. But Mr. Garrison, what do you mean by 'we?'"

"You had assumed I came here alone today?"

"That's what you told us."

"I told you nothing of the sort. That's what you wanted to believe. You see, the both of you have a problem: you believe whatever you want, despite overwhelming evidence to the contrary. You have no regard for the law or the peace that we so tenuously maintain. You allowed your daughter to learn by believing your eyes failed you. You broke the law by leaving her—and not reporting her in the first place—because you believed it would end poorly for you if you did otherwise. You believed you could escape your burden and hide in the Seltan plains where no one would come looking for you. And lastly, you believed me when I told you we would not hold you responsible for the crimes of your daughter."

"What are you trying to say?"

"James Howell Landen and Savana Shendal Rhome, you are under arrest for your crimes against our nation. You willingly allowed a daughter of the Silent Order—*your* daughter—to be educated. You purposefully ignored signs that your daughter was learning and took no steps to stop her. You also failed to report her crimes to the authorities, instead running away to hide. You have endangered everything we live for on Merced, and for that you will serve a life sentence in jail."

"Savana, run, I'll fend him off!"

"It's of no use. Again, I am not here alone. The exits are covered by half a dozen men each. It would be best if you were compliant—there's less pain involved that way. Oh, and I almost forgot, thank you for being so forthcoming with your crimes today. This would have been much more difficult for me had you said nothing or lied. I was working off complete hearsay and had no proof of anything. Your dimwittedness abounds. So thank you for that."

"What about Isaac and Eunice? They're the ones that taught her. They're the ones you want."

"James, I appreciate your candor and will note your incriminating words in the official files on Isaac and Eunice. I'm certain we will be bringing them in as well."

RE: RE: We have taken Landen and Rhome

Excellent work, Garrison. You know what to do next.

~ Ward

CHAPTER 12
THE PLAN

It's two weeks until my birthday. Two weeks until we finally get to make a plan. How do we upend this world that pits society against a group of silent, loving people? How do we free the August Children from the grasp of the Patricians? That's what we will start working on as soon as I am legally an adult—eighteen years old.

Ari and I train every morning, though our fervor has diminished a bit. The *knowledge of the possible* is a great concept, but it doesn't work so well when the final outcome is actually unknown. We pretended for years that we believed walking on the wind was possible. Now, though we don't admit it out loud, we know it is not. We haven't seen a large gain in two years. Since then we've been trying to simplify our motions.

For our first shifting trial in the morning we practice natural movements that we can do with a moment's notice. With her arms hanging at her sides, Ari flicks both hands outward, creating a gust of wind that can knock someone over if they aren't expecting it. Her precision and nonchalant body language are impressive. My turn. Standing in the same position Ari had, I flick my wrists up to send a shield of air rushing past my face. It forms a triangle, angling outward. The goal is to deflect a fist, or at least alter its trajectory to a more favorable location than one's nose. We don't typically name our moves, but I decided this one must be called, "Not in the face."

"Why call it that?"

"Tell me you're going to punch me."

With conviction that worries me a little, Ari flatly says, "I'm going to punch you."

"Not in the face! Not in the face!" Both of my arms shroud my head.

"Oh, I see," she says while giving me a light backhand to my stomach, "it's the cowards move."

"Hey, as long as I don't get hit in the face I'm fine with any label you want to give me." I give a toothy grin that highlights my fat lip. It pairs nicely with a week old black eye. Ari looks only slightly better than me.

For our second trial of the morning, we fight. Technically, it's more a game of tag; but we practice for the purpose of combat, should there ever be the need. Despite our inability to walk on the wind, our skills are quite substantial. We begin twenty meters apart. My goal is to touch Ari. That's it. She uses the wind to defend and tries to run away after her charge is spent. Only after she has spent her charge am I allowed to spend mine in an attempt to catch her. We switch places every day so we can practice both sides. We don't fight with wind at the same time, assuming that if we ever need to fight it won't be against another person with our unique skills. In the early days of fighting we were able to tag each other without shifting several times a week. It's been three months since I've tagged Ari without spending everything I have.

We used to only practice in the fort, but ever since Ari got her new identification we have been less concerned about practicing in the open. We both have our video mods active, so we can see if anyone is coming, but no one ever has. Even still, if someone sees us, it won't be a big deal. It would no longer be viewed as a clandestine meeting with the Silent Order—just a couple of young adults playing in the woods, making dust.

I grab a rock to throw at Ari. I can't be too far away, or she'll just run and I won't be able to catch her. If I'm too close she'll knock me off my feet. I use the trees for cover. My back presses against a large oak; Ari is now fifteen meters away over my left shoulder. She's not allowed to run until after I attack. I peel my right shoulder off the tree and continue to spin until I'm running directly at her. I'm only ten meters out. I throw the rock as hard as I can. We only aim for body shots. It's an easier target and we have enough visible bruises already. As I throw, I move to the right. She'll have to choose to stop me or stop the rock. Seven meters. Almost there. I'm leaning forward as I run, readying myself for the wind that is sure to knock me over if I'm not positioned properly. It doesn't come. Instead, she thrusts her arms down and a huge cloud of dust rises from the ground. I hear the thunk of the rock as it hits a tree. She must have dodged it. I can't see anything inside of the cloud. There's no point in stopping now. If I wait she'll run out the opposite side before everything has cleared. I don't know where she is, but my best chance is to try.

What would I do if I were in the center of the cloud? I wouldn't run the same direction as the attacker; that would allow them to keep their momentum as they follow after me. I would run the opposite direction, almost straight at them;

the turnaround time would be enough for me to get away. I know where a tree is on the opposite side of the cloud. I run through the center, not expecting to find Ari, but knowing it's the right move to make sure. Out the other side I take two steps up the side of the tree and propel myself in the opposite direction. Through the cloud and out again. Ari is only a few meters in front of me. I push as hard as I can, then dive. She sees it coming in her rear view and jumps to avoid my grasp. The tip of my finger brushes against her shoe.

"I tagged you!"

As Ari whips her head back to glare at me, I shift everything I have towards her feet. I did tag her, but that's not how you win the game. She's still running and expects she's won. The gust knocks her feet out from under her, and she lands squarely on her back.

"Ow! You did not tag me!"

"My finger brushed your shoe."

"That doesn't count! You have to actually stop me."

"I just meant that neither one of us had done that in a while."

"You just decided to *share*? Well, it didn't stop me."

"Yeah, but I stopped you, didn't I?"

"Doesn't count, I was dist-" Being distracted would be a losing argument. "Well, brushing my shoe doesn't count. And you haven't exactly tagged me now. You've only knocked me over. Draw."

"I can deal with a draw." It's more than fair. "I still tagged you."

Ari gives me a skeptical look, but doesn't say anything, knowing it will only incite me further. We both pick ourselves up off the ground and begin our walk home. We ditched the flying suits years ago after realizing it was nice to have some time to walk and talk, though today begins in silence. Not strained silence—this one is peaceful. Sure, we're both still a little riled up from the fight, but that's just the surface. We run deeper than that.

"Tell me something I don't know." Non-sequiturs are Ari's favorite.

"Sometimes when I look in the mirror I still expect to see someone else."

"That has to be a little rough. What *do* you see when you look in the mirror?"

"Confidence. Insecurity. I know the two don't exactly go together, but everything in life is complex. The face is what really throws me off. I expect the weathered and worn face I wore as the result of a long and wonderful life. I'm a little sad sometimes that I can't see that face any more. I don't even have any pictures. That was the face that watched over the people I loved most dearly. I'm not him, but sometimes I want to be—just for a moment—to remember everything that was. It's hard to let go. I was that person for so long, but now when I look in the mirror I see youth. I'm only just making my mark on this face. He needs a bit more experience. There's no character to it yet. It's less round than it was when I was just a boy, but it's still just as red on my cheeks. I do miss not having to shave every day. That was nice for a spell."

"What? You don't want to show off the bald patches on your face?"

"I'm sure it will be a fashion statement someday, but for now I think it's best if I stick with the clean look."

"Ok, now do me. What do you see when you look at me?"

I see my future. "Strength. Determination. Beauty." Why did I say "beauty" aloud? Bad move. How do I fix it? "And freckles. Freckles everywhere. You have so many freckles! Have you ever tried counting them? I'm sure you have thousands. Maybe just the ones on your face. How many freckles do you think you have on your face?"

Ari's face turns red. She is a little embarrassed by just how many freckles she has. I have always thought they make her prettier, but no telling her that right now.

"I likely have more freckles than you have hairs on your face."

"Are you questioning my manhood?"

"Heavens, no!" She gasps, covering her mouth with her hand.

"Sarcasm does not become you."

"Nor does manhood you."

Our conversation ends abruptly as we near the house. Something isn't right. I can't quite put a finger on it. I realize that I've slowed down. Ari is half a stride in front of me. I place my hand on her shoulder and we stop. Immediately, seeing my face in her rear view, she understands that something is wrong; but she doesn't know what it is either. Is it the sound? Yes, the sound. Pods are very quiet, but they do make a minimal amount of noise. One must have pulled up at the front of the house. Maybe several based on the low hum I hear. I sign as much to Ari. We can see the house. It's only 100 meters away. The vastness of the forest hides us from anyone who would give a cursory scan. I increase the opacity on my video feeds just a little bit. I don't want to miss any movement behind me. The back door of the house opens and I see Father walk outside with a Patrician.

"Elias, Elias, wherefore art thou?" He's nearly yelling, addressing the forest at large, "Betwixt the brevities of life we must eat, and the servants have preparethed the food." We come back at exactly the same time every day. Father knows this very well. He's specifically telling us not to come home.

"We should fight," I sign.

Ari turns slightly so I can see her hands, remaining focused on the house. "How many Patricians are there?"

I don't know. She doesn't know. It's the obvious question.

"Five…yes, fight," she continues. "Ten? Maybe. More? Definitely not."

"I think there's several pods out front, and they're looking for us now. At minimum there would be four, one for each of us. But it's likely there's eight or more."

"We can't, Eli. I know you want to, but we can't. If they find out you're of August, we're all dead. If they find out your family has been educating me, we're all dead. If they see us shift the wind…we're not wind walkers, but I can't imagine they would be pleased to find out we can lay waste to a room full of armed men with the wave of an arm. Even if we escaped they would hunt us."

My heart is racing. I can barely breath. Everything in me wants to scream and fight, but I am not allowed. I see Father turn to the Patrician, voice still blaring above the soft hum of the pods. "Do you hear that, sir? The silence, it calls to me. The vast emptiness of the forest receives my voice and I doth go forth into it as it calls me with silence." It's all complete nonsense, at least to the Patrician who is becoming visibly angry even from our vantage point 100 meters away. But the message Father gives us is exactly what we need: leave for Evanwood and the Silent Order. This is it. We are never going home again. Have we been beaten already? Certainly, if we stay. We have to go. Now.

Without a single word, Ari and I move in unison, slowly retreating from our position. We have to follow the plan. Father always told us he would make sure to give us a clear signal if something went wrong. No signal could be clearer than this. Once we can no longer see the house through the forest we move quickly to the tree that holds our suits. We've slimmed them down since originally making them. Now they fit comfortably under our clothes; the chaps bend at the knees so we can walk easily; and we no longer have helmets, but a simple visor—small enough to fit in a pocket—to protect our eyes. Time is of the essence, so we fasten everything on the outside and fly to our hideout as fast as we can.

We don't care if anyone finds the fort; this is just where our directions begin. Thirty paces east. Forty-five paces north. We now stand at the beginning of our escape route. This route was programmed the same as other paths that allow us to fly, with one key difference: the code disappears a few minutes after use. Mother created a loop in the code, keeping it in place until a specific condition is met. The condition is use. Once the path has been used the loop is broken. The next line begins a ten-minute countdown until all of the code is erased. The extra time allows for Ari and I being separated. Fortunately, that is not the case. We will go together; and once we are through, there will be no evidence that we were ever here. It's unlikely that someone would check the code of all the trees in the surrounding forest, but it's best not to doubt the overbearing nature of the Patricians; better to be safe. Ari and I turn towards each other and give a reassuring nod. This is what we are supposed to do. This was the plan for if everything went wrong, and everything has gone wrong. We don't discuss anything. There is no need. This is our only realistic option. We talked about everything at great length with my parents. This is the plan. We have to go. We have to go! In turn, we each step forward and fly.

After nearly an hour we arrive at our first destination: an open field fifty kilometers due north. It's just over a hectare in size, standing at the edge of a large ravine. The ravine is thirty meters deep and twenty meters across. A river may have flowed through it at one time, but it's just rock at the bottom now. Trees surround the clearing on the other three sides. Walking through the knee-high grass is a nice reprieve from flying. This place is peaceful, calming. The wind bends the grass in every direction. The current here is strong.

"Time for the next step." Ari's voice breaks my trance. "We need to move."

"Should we have waited longer?" Panic.

"How much clearer could your father have been, Eli?"

"I know, but maybe we could have helped—maybe we could have snuck them away with us."

"We did as we were instructed to do."

"But what if we could have done more?"

"Eli, we had no idea what the situation was. We have to trust that your father knew what was best. We made the right call."

"Yes, but they're *my* parents!" And of course they are hers now too, but the damage is done.

Ari doesn't make a sound—doesn't flinch—doesn't bat an eye. Tears stream down her face but she holds my gaze with a quiet, solemn composure.

"Ari, I'm sorry. I didn't mean to...I just...I'm sorry. Of course you understand exactly how I feel."

"You're an idiot," she says, wiping away the tears.

"Yes, I agree."

"Good, now that that's settled, It's time for the next step of our journey."

"Yes, follow the ravine west for four kilometers. Then we look for the track." The instructions are burned in my mind. I hated having to repeat them every day for two months, but Mother and Father were right about making us do it; we know exactly what to do. Now one foot in front of the other...move.

"It's beautiful here," Ari whispers. "We should stay forever."

"Definitely. Let's plant a tree in the center of the field and grow it into our new home." I could use a good diversion right about now.

"And whenever the wind dies down, we can practice shifting to send currents through the grass. It should never be still here."

"No one would ever find us. We could live until we are old without having to worry about a thing."

"It's settled. This is our new home. We will call it Paradise."

"Of course we will call it Paradise. That's its name. Why would we call it anything else?"

"I cannot think of a single reason."

We continue in silence as we pass through the rest of the field and into the forest. The trees are muted—the colors dull—the breaths that fill my lungs are barely enough to keep me moving. Save for a fleeting moment in Paradise, nothing about today is right.

"This is it."

I've been distracted for quite some time. Ari is right. This is our path. There is nothing that marks it as such, but it is obvious somehow. It just looks a little different than the rest of the forest around it. Were someone just passing by they might think it unique, or they might not notice it at all. I certainly didn't notice it, being as distracted as I am. It's good that Ari is here. I wonder where my parents are?

No one is following us; and, with several hours of travel ahead of us, we decide to spare a few minutes to find some food and put our suits on under our cloths. We have a plan; but things go wrong all the time, and we need to be at our best. Next stop: the Silent Order.

***

The village is the densest community I have ever seen. Homes surround a field maybe half the size of Paradise—it already feels like we were in Paradise a lifetime ago. A few trees are scattered through the open area, but they have all been formed to provide different needs of the community at large. This is where they gather. Homes do stretch further into the forest, but they are still far closer than anything I've seen here before.

We stand ten meters back from the edge of the clearing. We made it. This is where the plan gets hazy. We need to find someone and tell them who we are, but we have no idea who that is.

"Eli, what do we do now?"

"Tell them your name?"

"I guess that qualifies as an idea."

"Got another?"

"I have so many ideas, and they are all exceedingly better than yours; but I don't want to make you feel bad. So let's do your idea."

"I do have idea-based performance anxiety. So thank you." Nothing is safe. Everything is danger. Making jokes doesn't change that, but it does calm my nerves in advance of doing something stupid; and this definitely feels stupid. The Silent Order had once confirmed to the Patricians that Ari was here, even though she wasn't. If they could trust us enough to do that, we should trust them enough to announce our arrival. With a collective deep breath, we move forward.

I don't know how many people live here, but I get the feeling they all generally know what everyone looks like. At least that's what I assume based on the stares from children and adults as we enter the clearing. We are out of place. It's obvious. But we soldier on nonetheless.

A woman breaks away from a group of children to come greet us. Her brisk walk and the bobbing of her short hair says she is on a mission.

"Can I help you with something?" the woman says tersely.

We both stand silent. We agreed ahead of time that it would be best to limit what people know about us until we deem it safe. After a long enough pause, implying that we can't hear, Ari begins to sign.

"Hello, my name is Arielle-"

The woman raises her hand, stopping Ari in her tracks. She seems flustered, or possibly frustrated. "Quickly, come with me." She turns on her heels and heads for a large building, only turning back once to the group of children to sign that she has "taken care of it." I don't know what that means, but it seems to involve us. I don't feel like I'm in danger, but this is a little unsettling.

The woman obviously doesn't want to run, but the pace is uncomfortably fast. We're headed for a building at least twice the size of any of the houses we can see. It looks like it might be the place where normal people would check in on arrival. Maybe we should have scouted better and come to the main entrance. Too late now. The woman holds open a back door and we ascend a few steps up to the main floor.

The room has a few desks. It's a work area, but today it's empty aside from an agitated man pacing back and forth. We are only in the room moments before the woman from the field has made her way up and signs to the man. "This is Arielle."

He stops in his tracks and his face lights up. "Arielle, my name is David," he signs. "I have been in communication with Isaac and Eunice over the years. More on that later. Two patricians are in the adjoining room. They came here to check on you. I'm not sure what has happened, though I assume you'll fill me in when you get the chance. Right now, we need to present you to them. I was going to have someone else pose as you. Amera, here, was actually looking for the girl when she must have found you. Having the real you is much better. They want to be certain you've been here for the last seven years. They've been waiting for twenty minutes now. We should go in right away." His hands pause. "Except, we haven't had time to brief you on anything. You won't know how to answer any of their questions."

"Do they know how to sign?" Ari is calm, calculating.

"No, they have to speak through an interpreter. Amera typically interprets for me and will do the same for you as well."

Ari turns to Amera. "Do you know everything that goes on here and what my answers should be?"

"Yes, I suppose."

"Could you just answer for me? I will sign what I think my response should be, just in case either of them are able to understand any part. But then you can change my answers as needed."

The simplicity of the plan causes everyone to pause. Problems are not usually solved with such ease. Despite the lingering air of uncertainty, we proceed.

David looks to me. "You must be Elias."

I nod.

"It's probably best if you stay in here for the time being."

I have no intention of entering the other room, though it's good that we are all on the same page.

Through the wall I can hear the Patricians ask questions and Amera answer. Evidently Ari has been learning how to cultivate food, and she's been teaching children how to do some basic cleaning tasks. That's it. The patricians are happy to believe that Ari would be satisfied with doing only those two things for the last seven years. It's absurd. Their low opinion of the Silent Order clouds their judgement. It's nothing to be counted on, but we will use it to our advantage as long as it's useful. But they don't end there.

"We have some information regarding you learning under the influence of Isaac Jameson and Eunice Hall before you came to live here. This is criminal behavior. Do you have anything to say for yourself before we take you away?"

I recognize that voice…the slow drawl. Who is that? Doesn't matter now. Everything they asked about Ari's time here is just pomp and circumstance. They intend to take her away. I keep my hand on the door knob, readying myself to attack at a moment's notice. Peaceful resolution is best, but Ari will not be leaving here with the Patricians today no matter what.

After a longer pause than I am comfortable with, I finally hear Amera's voice again. "Do you see these bruises?"

Ari has bruises everywhere. So do I.

"In the seven years that I have been here," Amera continues, on Ari's behalf, "the Order has not ceased punishing me for my crimes. Isaac and Eunice were kind to me in some ways, but it served their ultimate purpose to see if they could educate me. They wanted to know just how much someone of the Silent Order could learn. They wanted to prove that we are still dangerous, believing that people have given us too many freedoms. They needed to show what one of us could become. So yes, I did learn, but it was under duress. Every week that I am here, I am brought in front of the children, and I tell my story. I tell them how I broke the law and how I deserve every punishment I receive. Then they have the children throw rocks at me and kick me. I would ask that you leave me here as a reminder to everyone: we are not to be educated; nothing good can come of it."

Ari is prepared to fight just as much as I am, but this lie is a thing of brilliance. It exonerates the motives of Mother and Father, makes the Silent Order sound like savages, and gives the Patricians a reason to leave her here. The bruises make it real for them; she appears to be trustworthy.

Everything that follows is surprisingly quick, especially considering that they are using an interpreter. The Patricians agree that Ari's punishment here is plenty and she will be a good reminder to the younger generation that they are not to learn. They think she's an idiot with no ability to fabricate a story. Luckily, they have no measure for their own incompetence.

"Thank you for cooperating," one of the Patricians says. It's one of the oddest phrases I've heard. It would be less odd if they meant what they said, but the subtext for the Silent Order is execution if they don't cooperate—not publicly, but certainly in some dark basement. No matter, the Patricians are gone.

David, Amera and Ari come back into the room I've been waiting in. Only Ari understands why I am so close to the door when they open it. The Patricians leaving is only a small victory, but it's far better than being defeated. We will take what we can get today.

"Hungry?" David beams a little smile at us. "Let's get some food and talk."

We leave the building and head towards the center of the field. A tree has been formed into an outdoor kitchen and eating area. Counters and sinks spread out from the base of the tree while the branches reach out ten meters before curling back to form tables and benches.

"Children here don't go to school," David tells us. "Instead, they become apprentices at very young ages and work with an adult until they have mastered the skills of their trade. They practice many trades throughout their childhood. Each trade happens to require some basic knowledge about math or science or history. As they get older the trades become more complex and require higher level thinking. We do not educate our children, but if they end up learning things from the trades required to keep our village running, who am I to stop that?" The twinkle in his eye says he helps facilitate this practice. "At meal times, they meet here to eat."

We stop at one of the tables. Meal time had finished hours prior, but there is plenty of food left over. A handful of adults and little apprentices are working on cleaning up and prepping for the next meal that would come in a few more hours. I watch for a moment to see what is being taught.

"Cooking basics, fractions, chemical reactions." David interrupts my silent pondering. "I'm sure a few other things are covered as well."

"Thank you, I was wondering."

The four of us sit down at the table, Ari and I sitting across from David and Amera. This is the first time I really have a chance to look at them. David appears to be almost fifty. He's tall...even sitting down he's tall. He also has a large smile. Amera is more restrained. Her body language is tense and uncomfortable. That makes me uncomfortable.

"Elias and Arielle," David speaks aloud for the first time. His voice is clear, unaffected.

"Eli and Ari are fine.". He knows who I am already, so I'm not giving anything away by speaking, but breaking the silence feels strange. "You can speak. You're not deaf, but you allow the Patricians to believe you are?"

"You are not deaf either, yet you chose to appear as a child of the Silent Order when you stepped in this field."

"It seemed safer that way."

"I agree. I was actually born here. My brother is deaf and my parents came here with him to live. Then they had me. I grew up learning how to sign as well as speak and am now the figurehead of the Silent Order, but I'll share more about that after you're both done eating so Ari can catch everything as well."

A few children bring out some food and set it in front of us. We waste no time.

"I can read lips," Ari signs poorly with a single hand as she balances an overstuffed sandwich in her other, "please continue."

"Perfect. Well, the Silent Order has no leader. We follow the teachings of Saree; and there is a group of men and women—our elders—who generally decide on important matters for our people. But everyone's voice, so to speak, is welcome. It's not a system of government. That would necessitate voting and pitting people against each other. Anyone can be a part of the group that makes decisions if they are willing to put in the time and effort to engage in radical discourse. And yes, we do make it sound a little more exciting than it is." He's lying. His dancing eyes say he thinks it's exactly that exciting; he's just a little embarrassed to say so. "I am a part of this group, but I also serve another purpose. The Patricians have an easier time understanding a group governed by a single person. That is nothing we desire, but we also understand the power they hold and the way they view us. So, for all intents and purposes, I am that man. I present myself as deaf and Amera translates everything for me. We've never had to use the trick you pulled today, Ari, but my ability to hear has let me understand situations better. Sometimes they will ask Amera not to translate something, or maybe they'll speak quietly to each other if Amera has to leave the room for a minute. It has provided me with a lot of insight into their reasons for coming here. For instance, today, as they were leaving, they said-"

"-that they thought this was a dead end to begin with—just tying up loose ends." Ari's single hand waves about, barely intelligible, eyes focused on her oversized sandwich. She's made a severe dent, but she seems determined to destroy it.

"You obviously have a few tricks up your sleeve," Amera says hesitantly, "their backs were turned when they said that."

Ari moves her wayward hand with devilish confidence. "I'm *very* good at reading lips...and body language too."

I understand she is being funny, mostly due to hunger and exhaustion, but both David and Amera's faces are colored with confusion. "We've traveled very far today and haven't eaten much. Ari's secrets are not mine to tell, but I would imagine that she will share them with you when she has reached a saner state of...stomach."

Amera glares across the table. David just chuckles and continues. "As you can understand, I keep my voice hidden in order to give myself more of an advantage when dealing with the Patricians. My position holds no power here, but it is important for appearances. I relay all the information to the other elders and we decide what to do with it together. I enjoy playing at being in charge, though I would never want to take on that role with these people. What we have here is unique.

"Now enough about me and what we do here. You have come for a reason. We laid a path for you years ago—at your parent's request— and now you are here. What brings you such a great distance, traveling alone?"

"As you well know by now, my parents have been taken by the Patricians."

David's face becomes somber. "We are very sorry about that. They are good people."

"Thank you. We were coming home and saw it from a distance. My father knew we would be back, so he was outside with one of them, rambling on about a number of different things in order to tell us what to do." I should sound confidant; not this wavering voice of an adolescent boy. I haven't thought about them all day. I just stuck to the plan and focused on that. No tears. No! Deep breath.

"It's ok if you need a minute."

I can't tell if David is patronizing or kind. I feel everything so strongly right now. "No, it's fine. My Father's words were mostly nonsense, but he made it clear that we should come here. This was always the plan if things went wrong. I don't know what happened except that somehow the Patricians learned my parents had taught Ari. I can only assume the 'dead end' they were referring to was their search for us here."

David nods in agreement. "That seems likely. And again, I'm so sorry about your parents."

"You don't sound surprised."

"To be honest, I'm not. We've known your parents for quite some time. Many years ago they came here to help us design some homes. The Patricians understood that we needed more sufficient housing or we would begin migrating to other areas. They had given us some rudimentary homes long ago, but every few years we had to make requests for additional homes and they would send someone to apply the code. It was decided that we should have some limited ability to create homes ourselves as we needed. No one likes visiting us, so this was a win for everybody. Your mother and father were the only ones willing to come and help. They essentially gave us a workaround for applying code. We don't have the same access to our CIs that you do, so they made tokens that could hold the code and apply it when it comes in contact with a tree. Isaac did try and find a way around the limitations of my CI. It took the better part of a day, but he figured it out. In the end, though, I decided it best to leave the settings in the CI alone.

"We were told your parents came begrudgingly, with some pressure placed on them, but it was just a ruse. They were kind to us. Isaac didn't know how to sign, but insisted we teach him. Eunice knew a bit already; she had a friend who was of the Order when she was young. Your parents wanted to know everything about us and told us they'd been waiting for years to come and meet us; they just needed a justifiable reason for their visit."

I can't think—I can't move—I can't speak. My parents are gone and I wasn't able to do anything about it. Focus. Listen to his words. "Why weren't you surprised they were taken?"

David's face becomes stiff. He was hoping I would let it go. "Quite frankly, they're careless. They seemed to have the same goals we did, but they would often put themselves in precarious situations. Even coming here, as they did, lacked requisite caution."

"They came here to help you!"

"I didn't say that we were unappreciative. You might notice that you came here today on a very long path that we laid out at their request. I'm only saying that they can tend towards carelessness in their pursuit of what is right."

"And you're here now. That is the first thing they would have wanted, right?" Amera's smile is not as comforting as she might hope. She can see that I am having a hard time, but she's simultaneously unhappy with our presence.

I nod in response. A few slow breaths and my heart rate returns to something reasonable.

"You mentioned having a plan," Amera prods. "What does this plan hold next for you? Focusing on what we know might help us solve problems surrounding things we don't know. At the very least, it can give you something to do. I'm so very sorry they took your parents, but we should move forward and figure out what comes next. What was the plan before all of this happened?"

"Come here. Hide. Live our lives? I don't know." It's a simple question. Why can't I answer it?

"Your voice tells me you're not interested in just living your lives here."

Amera is obviously not interested in us living our lives here. But if I'm honest, neither am I. "That is a very true statement. In two weeks, we were going to begin laying the groundwork for...our future." Vagueness seems appropriate here.

"And what would that entail?" Amera presses. "Full clarity here would be most advantageous so we can understand how best to help you."

And how best to get rid of us. No matter, she's right. Here goes nothing. "I guess our end goal would be to dismantle the rule of the Patricians."

Amera stifles a laugh. "And how exactly were the four of you planning on taking down a global organization?"

"I'll tell you in a little over two weeks?" My sheepish grin and shoulder shrug make everyone laugh a little. "I think our plan has changed though. First, we need to find my parents; then we can take over the world. It's important to do things in order." It feels nice to make a little joke. It doesn't fix anything, but it is cathartic.

Finally, sandwich finished, Ari decides to join the conversation with two hands. "We haven't made any kind of plan yet. Like Eli was saying, we were going to start on his birthday in two weeks. Obviously, everything has changed. I assume the two of us will begin planning tomorrow. There is no need to wait any longer. We would be grateful if we could stay here and hide, but it is completely understandable if that brings too much danger to your people. Oh, and thank you for the sandwich. It was delicious!"

"You're welcome for the sandwich," David laughs, "and you may certainly stay here, but I have to ask, what kind of plan pits two people against thousands? That is not a war you can win. My family came here because living outside of this village was too much to handle. You must know firsthand how hard it is. Why don't you considered staying here permanently?"

Ari is not deterred in the least. "We don't intend to start a physical war. First, we will gather information. We have no idea where they took Isaac and Eunice. We need to find out. Once we have freed them, we need to find something about the Patricians that would ruin their credibility with the people of Merced. I don't know how we will find that information, but I think Isaac and Eunice will have some thoughts once we get them back.

"Right now, the Patricians hold influence with most people. They have convinced the masses that the Silent Order is...evil, for lack of a better word. We want to strip them of their influence. Then, all they will have is physical force, but using that force will turn people against them. No one will have their children evaluated at one month, August or otherwise. No one will respect the laws. We will unite. Then we will politely ask them to dismantle their oligarchy. If they don't comply, we start a real war," she smirks. "It's pretty simple when you think about it."

I can't tell if David is awestruck or dumbfounded. Maybe both.

"Ari, I...I don't have any personal issues with your plan, except for the starting a war part. The Silent Order will not ever be any part of something like that. We follow the teachings of Saree; peace is the only way forward for us. If you do end up staying here—which I believe would be the best thing for you—it would behoove you to understand that; we are not a violent people.

"Now, I don't know exactly what you're looking for, but any information that would ruin the credibility of the Patricians exists only in Suvault. There is virtually no way of accessing records of that nature. Unfortunately, that is also where you would find information on the location of Isaac and Eunice. I would strongly recommend against any attempt to find the information you seek. They kill members of the Silent Order that enter Suvault. It is not a place for a deaf person."

"I think I can manage." Ari says sweetly. Her voice is perfect. I couldn't have said it more clearly myself.

Both David and Amera sit up straight, eyes wide. David clears his throat before speaking. "I was certain you were of the Silent Order. That's what Isaac and Eunice led us to believe, at least. What is your ploy here? Why are you pretending? I mean, I guess I do the same thing, but it is for a very specific purpose. What is the purpose of your disguise? And who are you, if not Arielle Linivette SO?"

"You have things mixed up," Ari continues in a charming tone. "You can hear, but you pose as someone of the Silent Order. For me, it's just the opposite. I am of the Silent Order, but I pose as someone who can hear."

"You can obviously hear," Amera spits. "That's very clear to all of us."

"No, I pose as someone who can hear."

David is slowly clenching and unclenching his fists below the table. He doesn't like this. "I've heard deaf people vocalize before," he says. "Your voice gives you away; you are not the same. I don't understand what you're getting at. Explain yourself or we are done here!"

Ari looks over at me from the corner of her eyes, her face a bit smug. She gives a tiny shrug. It's my turn to explain. "I promise, we are not trying to deceive you. May I tell you a story that should help clear things up?"

"By all means," David says half sarcastically, waving an exasperated arm.

Deep breath. Here goes nothing.

CHAPTER 13
SECRETS

RE: Jameson/Hall in custody

There was no sign of the girl or the boy. We're still looking. So far, the parents won't say anything. Or, more precisely, they won't say anything coherent. They keep blathering on with nonsense and calling each other Romeo and Juliette. It's fine though, we'll employ our more…advanced interrogation techniques once I return.

I took a short trip to Evanwood. I wanted to see the SO girl with my own eyes. None of this feels right and that was a thread I could follow up on easily. I considered taking her into custody as well, but it became obvious that she is beaten regularly by the other members of SO for her crimes of learning. She has bruises everywhere. I just couldn't bring myself to free her from that sweet, sweet justice.

The SO girl did spill everything she knew about Jameson and Hall. She claimed they were educating her to make a point that the SO were still dangerous. I believe she may have been told that. I still don't know what the true motives of Jameson and Hall were.

~ Garrison

RE: RE: Jameson/Hall in custody

I am impressed with your attention to detail. You certainly leave no stone unturned.

The SO complain about being oppressed, but they are every bit as awful as we have always known they are. It's amazing how deluded they can become. Sounds like the SO girl is getting every bit of what she deserves. No need to sully your hands with her further.

As far as the boy and girl are concerned, keep looking. It's likely they have been indoctrinated to believe some things that aren't true about us. They're probably scared. We should be understanding with them as long as they cooperate. I can't imagine they've gone far. Use whatever resources necessary.

~ Ward

"There are four people in the world that know who Ari and I truly are: my parents and the two of us. We are in need of your help and your trust, so today that number will grow to six. I would ask that you leave it at that. David, I understand that you are not the actual head of the Silent Order, but you have made a point to receive us. Amera, it seems that your position here is intertwined with David's and it would not be prudent to leave you in the dark. I also understand that we are in no position of power. We come to you asking for much and offering very little. So, I will ask you at the end of my story if it is something you can refrain from sharing with others. I believe that you will deem our secrets worthy of being kept."

"To the extent that I can," David says slowly, "I will keep any secret you tell me. "If I cannot, I will tell you. Amera?"

"I will keep any secret David does. It's not my place to be spreading gossip."

"Thank you. Both of you have been gracious in receiving us and feeding us, and even hiding us from the Patricians, though I guess Ari did present herself; but you still hid the truth of the situation.

"First, let me tell you about Ari. I met Ari when she was four years old. She could not speak. She could not hear. Someone here, I'm assuming you, David, knew of her and asked my mother to check in on her. Life is very difficult for deaf children who do not live in this village, as you well know. At four years old, Ari was not interested in deceiving anyone. She hid nothing from us. She was desperate to learn, so we took her in. I would wager a large sum that Ari's intellectual prowess is exactly the same as children of August. She doesn't have the knowledge of a past life to draw from, but the rate at which she learns is phenomenal. She learned to vocalize. Later, my father gave her auditory mods. They didn't fix her hearing, but it allowed us to create a program to turn speech into text. Anything you say comes up on her display."

"So that's how you knew what they were saying when their backs were turned!" Amera almost shouts.

Ari just smirks and shrugs her shoulders as if she has won a game.

"Once we completed the speech program, we also created an audio analyzer. We used that to help compare and contrast Ari's speech to others'. She adjusted the shape of her mouth and sounds she was making until they matched everyone else. As time passed and she got better, I would identify small issues for her, then she'd practice, practice and practice some more. Now we have reached a point where she doesn't sound any different than someone with full hearing."

David is stunned—his face almost stuck in place with shock. "That is simply amazing. I never would have dreamed of someone doing that. Ari, why is it that you choose to have Eli share this instead of sharing yourself? There's nothing wrong, I just want to...I want to understand everything!"

"I come across as much more impressive and humble when someone else tells my story." She almost says it without laughing. "Truthfully, I'm tired. I also like hearing Eli tell my story. It's fun to have someone else share how special you are. I think it also holds a little more weight when someone else shares something improbable about me. It's more readily believable. How do you feel about my chances in Suvault now?"

"Obviously, they are much better than before. It's still not safe to go there, and I have no idea how you would get what you're looking for. I honestly don't believe I could condone such a mission, but I am willing to hear your plan come together and share my thoughts. You've proven that you are nothing if not resourceful. You deserve, at the very least, an open ear."

"Do you have something in mind that will stand in our way? I know there will be a lot of complications Ari and I will have to deal with, but you seem to think we would automatically fail."

David breathes deeply through his nose. His chest raises high and slowly falls. Bad news. "Any information you would want is in the Hall of Records."

"Well that's great news! One planning point down. We know where to go." Ari places a check mark on an invisible piece of parchment. "We will not be deterred by difficulty. I am speaking to you in perfect English. You understand how much work went into this. We are determined, but we can also handle bad news."

"Thank you for your candor. I'll explain. To get into the Hall of Records you have to register at the entrance with your ID. I'm certain that both of you are on a watch list by now and would be flagged immediately on entry. That's your first problem. The main floor contains information everyone is allowed to access. As you get higher in the building, the information becomes restricted and there are security clearances that have to be passed. Sometimes it's just a code, and we do have sympathizers in Suvault who can help get the codes; but more often it's something else. The higher the floor, the higher the security clearance you need. Every route to the highest floor, which is where you'd want to go, requires an access code as well as knowledge of Earth. Questions are asked that only the highest-ranking officials and those of August know the answer to. Unfortunately, we do not have any contacts with that kind of clearance. We've encountered some of the questions, but they are nonsense." David alters his voice, speaking slowly, as if he is reading off a screen, "What happened to the three blind mice?"

"The farmer's wife cut off their tails." Ari rattles off matter-of-factly.

"Exactly." David doesn't understand. "It's just nonsense. Who knows what the answer is?"

"No," Ari says deliberately, "the farmer's wife cut off their tales. That's the answer. It's a nursery rhyme from Earth."

Amera, looking frustrated, decides to try her hand at explaining. "I think what David is getting at is that you can make up whatever answer you want, which you are obviously good at, but there's no way to know if you're right; and since there are seemingly infinite answers, there's no realistic way to be correct. For example, we know there were billions of people on Earth. One question asked who the most hated person on Earth was. Even if you knew the names of every person, your odds of guessing correctly would be statistically impossible; and we don't even know the names."

My turn. "Easy, it's Michael McClellan. He worked at a nuclear power plant during the middle of the twenty-first century. Nuclear power wasn't always stable or safe at the time, but if managed properly it can power massive cities. Michael McClellan was a technician who worked in the control room of one of these power plants. He fell asleep on the job. When he awoke, the power plant was melting down...which, I guess, is a bit of an odd phrase. Suffice it to say the power plant had become...unstable and no longer safe for anyone within several kilometers. Despite shutting down everything he could, Michael was not able to stop the catastrophic end. Long story short, millions of people died. Michael, himself, made it out alive and lived for a few years before dying of radiation poisoning. Now, you have to understand, this definitely wasn't the worst thing that ever happened on Earth, nor was he actually the worst person on Earth; but he became a part of popular culture. His name ended up being synonymous with everything that was wrong with our society and planet. Natural disasters? Newscasters would report that Michael McClellan had fallen asleep in the control station again. Car accident? Michael McClellan fell asleep at the wheel. War? Michael McClellan drifted off and forgot to keep the peace. It was a huge mistake he made, and it cost a lot of lives; but he didn't quite deserve the infamy his name was elevated to."

Amera and David stare blankly at me. They are speechless. A child of August has not visited the Silent Order in hundreds of years. This is something new.

Finally, Amera manages *some* words. "You can't be..."

Ari waits a few long moments before completing her sentence, "...a child of August? Why, yes, he is. We are quite the dynamic pair," she beams.

David finally breaks out of his stupor. "And that's why you have such a clear memory of when Ari came to your family. These are not stories you heard from your parents; these are things you experienced firsthand."

"Yes."

His pace quickens. "And when you said that Ari is the intellectual match for a child of August you meant that she is *your* intellectual match."

"Precisely."

"How? How are you here right now? How did your parents keep you for so long? Do you think this has anything to do with the Patricians taking them away? Do they know about you? This is your secret! This is why you asked for my discretion in keeping your secret. Oh my! Yes, of course, we won't tell anyone! But how?"

"The short version is that my parents helped me trick the Patricians when I was a baby. After that I just had to act like a small child whenever anyone else was around. They educated both Ari and me. They wouldn't start planning to fight the Patricians until I turned eighteen. They were determined that each of us would have a reasonable childhood, and being a legal adult carries plenty of benefits when trying to dismantle an oligarchy. To my parents' credit, I wouldn't change anything they did.

"I don't know why the Patricians took them. Our only lead is that the Patricians found out my parents were teaching Ari. I don't know if they're also aware of my nature, though I would venture a guess they are not. I don't think the situation would have appeared as civil as it was if they knew I was of August. And there would have been a lot more infantry. I could be wrong, but it doesn't hurt anyone to venture a guess."

"I have never met anyone quite like the two of you. Thank you for trusting me—and trusting Amera—enough to share your secrets with us. I will not share them with anyone else, but I would urge you to share your plan—whatever you have—with the elders tomorrow evening. We gather every week for discourse and stories—which happens to be tomorrow—and you should present your ideas then. I don't think your desires, aside from war in the distant future, are out of line with the values of the Order. Nor do I believe you intend to put us in danger. I still don't see how you would be capable of completing your mission; but at this point—with all the revelations you have shared—I must suspend my disbelief and allow you an opportunity to share. If it is reasonable for us to help, I believe we will."

***

"The elders are not specifically old, nor are they a fixed group of people," Amera explains as we walk towards the gathering. "If anyone in the Silent Order wants to be an elder, they must simply say so at a gathering and be nominated by ten others. Young, old, women, men, anyone who wants a voice in steering the Order can be an elder. All voices are heard, and differing opinions encouraged. It was no slip of the tongue that David called it ‘discourse.’ Their weekly tradition is to gather and do just that. Sometimes there are important things to discuss and they work through the problem from every angle. No one moves forward until they fully understand the intention and meaning of the opposing view; no one chooses how to solve a situation without discussing it. There is no maximum number of elders. The fewest we have ever had was seven, the most was twenty-three. No one has to vacate a seat in order for someone else to take one. The group takes as many people as it needs to have. While we are one people, when you have so many, it is natural for smaller sects to form. If any sect needs a voice, they nominate someone to be a part of the elders. Every person is to be represented and heard. This is the group you will present your case to. No better opportunity will come your way.

“When there are no pressing issues to discuss, the elders share stories with anyone who comes to listen. Some of the stories are about our history, others about Saree, and many more are fables and children’s tales. I’m not sure if we will have stories today or not. Part of that depends on how well your ideas are received.

“As you can see up ahead, fifteen elders sit on the far side of the fire. It serves as our only light this evening. As I am unaware of your education on such things, you may or may not know that fires aren’t especially common on Merced, mostly because of a lack of wood. There are laws that forbid harvesting trees.”

This is the nicest Amera has been, but the condescension is not lost on me. We will let her continue on since neither of us seem motivated to engage her in conversation. It’s easier this way.

“This fire is made with discarded branches. Trees do, in a sense, prune themselves when they need to in order to foster growth in other areas. Members of the Order gather these fallen branches every week to make a fire. Tomorrow morning they will gather the ashes from the pit and return them to the trees as fertilizer. They will thank the forest for the wood and help it to grow and become even greater. Most people generally respect the nature of fires and the significance they hold, but the Order has a special connection with the forest and treats it with reverence. We are oxpeckers on the back of a giant elephant." Her smug smile makes it clear she knows a little bit about Earth; Merced has many animals, but oxpeckers and elephants are not among them.

Amera continues explaining everything as we arrive. With how nervous I feel, it's a welcome distraction. "About three hundred tonight; aren't the two of you special. When important issues are being discussed there will typically be about a hundred that come to listen. They, in turn, will report back to smaller groups what was said. Not everyone is able to attend, but the information circulates quickly and no one is left in the dark. News of your arrival has spread especially fast. A group of this size at an elder meeting is almost unheard of; but Eli, your parents were well liked, so everyone is concerned about their wellbeing."

Ari gives in and asks the question Amera has been waiting to hear. "Why aren't you a member of the elders?"

"How sweet of you to suggest such a thing, but I don't need to be. I have never disagreed with a decision they have made. Certainly, I have had my reservations or felt differently about something myself, but not once have I been able to discount their logic or their concern for our people. I am represented well by the minds that currently sit in those seats. If that ever changes I will nominate myself, but I don't foresee that happening any time soon."

As we walk into the light of the fire every eye turns in our direction. There is silence as we pass through the throngs of people; a stillness and quiet that is more intense than what is to be expected. We make our way to the center with only the fire standing between us and the elders.

David stands from across the fire to address us and the crowd. He signs tonight. "Thank you for coming here tonight. We have some special guests here with us." He looks directly at us. "I have shared a few details with the elders about who you are, enough that they have agreed to hear you tonight, but why don't you share your story with us all."

Ari told me that I would be speaking tonight; no point in making a nervous decision in the moment. But we hadn't counted on the circular setup. It is fine for the elders since everyone else can see them, but we stand in the center. It is the elders who need to hear our story the most, but it is unfortunate that many who are directly behind us will miss what is being said. Evidently, Ari is thinking the same exact thing. She takes a single step forward and turns 180 degrees. Now she is facing me, offset by just a meter, hands at the ready. She will repeat everything I share so everyone can see. Ha! As if Ari will actually repeat my words. She will tell the same story, but she'll change anything she feels like changing. You cannot silence Ari; her voice will always come through.

"Thank you for hearing our story. My name is Elias Jameson Hall. I am the son of Eunice Hall and Isaac Jameson." Hundreds of feet stomp the ground once in unison. I feel it in my toes. What does this mean? I don't want to offend, but the faces I see are attentive and welcoming. "Some of you remember them." They nod. Good. "They came here and helped you design your homes many years ago. Standing next to me is Arielle Linivette SO.

She is a daughter of Saree." Two stomps. The deaf who are abandoned are called children of Saree. The Order honors them to help ease their pain. This is going better than I expected. "Ari has lived with my family and me for the last eleven years. Seven years ago, at my parent's request, you agreed to say that she lived here with you, despite the fact that she did not. We cannot express our gratitude enough. You have granted her a life that no one could have imagined would be possible for her. We came here yesterday on a path you created for us. My mother and father were taken by the Patricians. We were not home when they came, and my father made certain we were aware of the situation before we arrived, so we ran. We knew this was a place of safety, so this is where we came. Now we seek to rescue them, but we do not know how."

Ari presses forward as I pause. Of course she would do that. No time to gather my thoughts; I repeat her now.

"We came here because we do not believe the Silent Order attacked the Patricians in The Uprising. That is the narrative they want people to believe because it is convenient for them. Though we may not know how yet, we intend to expose this truth. We intend to start a war of words; we will attack the lies the Patricians tell—we will attack the bigoted treatment of those in the Silent Order—we will attack the idea that children of August should be taken from their families. We will fight for truth. We will fight for compassion. We will fight for families to live freely, without discrimination. This is our war. We shared this with David, and he asked us to share with you. So, we stand before you today seeking the wisdom of Saree. Grant us that and we shall be forever grateful."

"But before we can do any of that, we need to find my parents. They will help lead the charge in exposing the truth. We have no means of even knowing where they are.

The Order is bound to have more resources than we do. We ask for your help in finding them."

As Ari finishes repeating my last words, she turns to face the elders. An older man, possibly in his seventies, stands in order to be seen by all.

"My name is Salvo, and I am very glad you came here to be with us today." His face resides in contentment. His light smile emphasizes the wrinkles that already cut deeply through his skin. His history is happiness, each wrinkle earned with years of joy. While he signs, he also hums lightly. It's pleasant and warm. For me, it gives a voice to his hands.

"Arielle, may I ask you something about what you shared?" He is aware that Ari had taken over in the middle of our speech, despite the fact that he could only see what I had signed. Ari nods.

"Have you ever read *The Silence of Saree*?"

"At least 100 times."

"And do you remember how it ends?"

"Of course. 'This is the history that is known'."

"Good. Now, is there anything that is odd concerning the punctuation?"

"There's no period at the end." Ari reads more carefully than I do. I've never noticed that.

"Why do you think that is?"

"I had always assumed that Bometir was trying to punctuate his last line by the lack of a period. It's a statement that needs no end. What Saree built will not end. Her legacy remains."

"That is an excellent interpretation. I agree with you that Saree's legacy will continue throughout time, and it should. But let me suggest that the ending is something different.

"Many people knew that Alfred Bometir had come to speak with Saree. There was an expectation that he would write about their encounter. Had nothing been written it would have been concerning to the masses, so we were given *The Silence of Saree;* but it's not complete. Saree shared much more with Alfred, and we believe he wrote more."

"And how do you know this?"

"We are not allowed to catalog anything. Everyone here learns to read and write, though we do not allow the Patricians to know that."

Several of the elders are visibly uncomfortable, increasingly so the longer Salvo shares. Why?

"Calm yourselves," Salvo says, addressing the other elders. "They have shared some of their secrets with us tonight. There is nothing to fear in sharing some of ours with them." He turns back to Ari. "As I was saying, the most the Patricians are aware of is that David is capable of some clerical writing. That is it. If we wrote down our histories they would be found and destroyed. Then we would be punished for our transgressions. So we don't write anything down. Instead, we tell stories. We meet weekly for discourse, but rarely do we have much to discuss. Even when we do, it often goes quickly; and we end up with plenty of time to share our tradition. I memorized the stories I was told when I was young, and I have taught them to every child who will listen. This is our history. For hundreds of years this is what we have done, and when I was young I was told this about *The Silence of Saree*: 'This is the history that is known until now.' This was the beginning of what Alfred truly desired to share. He spoke with Saree at length and included a transcript of their conversation in *The Silence of Saree.* Unfortunately, he wanted to cross check some of the details he had been given, so he went to the Patricians to ask about it. He assumed he would find answers. What he found was death. Not immediately. His history had to be published first, redacted, of course. He died a short time after. We have stories of what their conversation held, but I don't think those are important right now. No one will believe a story told by the Silent Order. What someone would believe is the words of Alfred Hugo Bometir. If you desire the wisdom of Saree, this is what you should be looking for."

"And how do we find it?"

"The Patricians are too meticulous to discard any document. They keep records of everything to catalog their success and remember how they came to power. While they may no longer have the original document, I'm certain a copy would be kept in the Hall of Records. I do not have any ideas about how you might obtain such a thing without being caught; but I suspect you have a few secrets that might allow you to imagine more success than I; and for me, that is enough."

"That's enough stories for now, Salvo," another elder scolds.

Salvo is already sitting; he is done anyhow. Someone just felt the need to make it look like they have the ability to silence him. He obviously can't be silenced, though his advice doesn't seem to be of use to our immediate aims. What's his angle?

The elders confer amongst themselves. The silence feels unnatural to me—unnerving, even. Is it any more silent now than it was before? After several minutes David stands to address everyone.

"Eli and Ari, we will gladly shelter you and provide you with food. You may stay here as long as you like...become a part of our community, even."

I've heard him offer this before. It's pageantry, now, that David is after.

"As to your...other desires, we are unsure of our ability to help you. A few of us will meet with you in the morning to discuss with you in further detail."

The only thing I can do is nod in agreement. No point in arguing. The elders don't want to make a scene in front of the people; if I made one it would only satiate my desires—it would not help in rescuing my parents.

With nothing else on their agenda, the rest of the evening is for stories. Salvo is the story teller tonight. Of course he is.

"This is the story of The Keeper," Salvo begins, "first told by Saree centuries ago."

Only a few moments in and I am captivated by the gentle hum of his voice and the eloquent movement of his hands. It's calming; just what I need. Within his fluid motion, I no longer see Salvo, but the story he tells.

Two young men travel through the woods: Feresh and Somosh. They are companions, but when they come to a fork in their path they cannot agree which direction they should go. They decide it is best to rest for the night and make a decision in the morning. They enjoy each other's company throughout the evening and agree it would be best if they could continue on together, but when morning comes they still cannot agree.

Out of the bushes crawls a small child wearing clothes made of large green leaves. He appears not to have reached his seventh year, but he speaks with the confidence of a full-grown man.

"I am The Keeper," the boy declares. "Do you seek my assistance?"

"What are you the keeper of?" Feresh questions. "We cannot know if we need your assistance without knowing what it is that you keep."

"I am The Keeper of knowledge. My book can guide you through the darkest of times."

"We are simply stuck at this crossroads," Somosh shares with the boy. "We are not in need of knowledge. We just have to make a decision about which way to go."

"Perhaps you would like to know what lies down each path," The Keeper continues. "My book contains knowledge that could help you."

"Let us find out what lies down each path, Somosh," Feresh implores, but Somosh does not listen.

"I will go to the right," Somosh declares. "Feresh, you may come with me or choose your own path, but I am leaving now." And with that, he leaves.

Feresh, not wanting to spoil the wonder of seeing new things, asks this, "Keeper, I do not want to know exactly what I will find, but I want to know the way I should go. Does your book of knowledge tell you that?"

"The book tells me you should go to the left. To the right lies a barren wasteland. The left, though dangerous at times, holds the beauty you seek."

Feresh thanks The Keeper and proceeds to the left. On his travels, he encounters the most wondrous things. Flowers cover the forest floor. Rivers rage, threatening to pull him under as he crosses. Waterfalls spill into shimmering lakes. He climbs cliffs and traverses canyons on the smallest of fallen trees. The canopy above protects him from the harsh rays of the suns and presents him with delicious fruit as he has need. Going to the left was the best decision he ever made.

The story of Feresh reminds us that we should always choose to listen to knowledge. It can be dangerous, but it is a powerful tool and grants us the most fantastic opportunities.

Having chosen the path to the right, Somosh finds that the forest around him recedes quickly. A wasteland lies before him. Soon, everything crumbles around his path; and he walks with a cliff to either side. There is nowhere to find shelter or food. At the end of a very long day he stops to rest, exhausted from his travels. Just then, The Keeper appears in front of him, offering knowledge that would lead to a better path. This time Somosh does not disregard The Keeper and his book of knowledge, but takes his advice instead. Following a new path, Somosh finds Feresh and revels with him in the beauty of the land.

The story of Somosh reminds us that our mistakes are not permanent and knowledge will always present itself to us. It is our responsibility to overcome our pride and accept the help we need.

The last flame of the fire flickers out as Salvo finishes the story. We stand, warming our hands by the embers, waiting until only three of us remain: myself, Ari and Salvo. We need Salvo. I don't know why, but somehow, I just know. I glance at Ari. She gives a single nod of approval.

"Salvo, if we were to share with you what you might consider secrets, would you be willing to help us imagine a plan?"

"I would be delighted! But I am an old man and could use a rest. Can it wait until the morning?" he smirks.

"Certainly. We are grateful for your help."

"Of course. Now, would you indulge me in a curiosity before we call it a night?" Salvo's eyes dance in the darkness. "Would you put this fire out?"

"I'd be happy to. Do you have water I can fetch from somewhere?"

"Not with water." His eyes flit around. No one else is anywhere nearby. He leans in and whispers with his hands, "Can you put it out with the wind?" He asks as if I might not understand. How could he know? It doesn't matter. He is someone to be trusted—both Ari and I feel it.

I can feel the devilish grin spread across my face. One step closer to the fire pit now, the heat courses through my clothes. I can feel the burn as my skin touches the layers I'm wearing. With my right hand, palm facing down, I make a circle above the remaining coals. My left hand acts as a guide, helping constrain the wind, only allowing it to swirl over the pit. Fire, like flashes of lighting, spreads through the wind. I close my right hand in a tight fist and drop it in the center of the circle I created. Abruptly, I lift up and break my fist open and pull my arm back all together. A ten-meter spire of flame and wind erupts from the lowly embers. It lasts a single second, and then it's gone. The embers are all burnt out and only a trace of smoke remains.

"Magnificent," Salvo mutters with his hands, eyes transfixed on the fire that no longer exists. He stares straight ahead for several long moments. I'm certain the afterimage of the flame dances on his eyes in the same way it does on mine. As the afterimage subsides, he turns to look at us. "I had wondered if you could do this. Spectacular! Thank you. I will have more questions for you tomorrow, but I need to get my beauty sleep." With a wink and a smile, he hobbles off.

We follow suit; time for sleep.

CHAPTER 14
SALVO

RE: Elias Jameson Hall and the girl

I've been sending search parties in ever expanding circles looking for any trace of the boy and the girl. I have accounted for every pod in the vicinity. So far there is no trace of them. I will continue my search and update you when I have any new information.

~ Garrison

RE: RE: Elias Jameson Hall and the girl

Search parties are good. Keep your personal focus on the parents. The boy and girl will show up eventually. The most important piece was getting the parents, and you did that.

~ Ward

Ari is nearly bouncing out of her seat downstairs. They'll be here soon, and we have a game to play. She can't wait. I could use the diversion as well. This house we're in is comforting, but also eerie. Several parts of it are identical to our own home. I expect to see Mother and Father come around the corner at any moment, a constant reminder that we need to figure out where they are and specifically why they've been taken. Is the Order actually going to help us? Our story making it here feels inspiring, but it's not exactly in line with the calculated risks the people here traditionally take.

"They're here!" Ari calls from downstairs.

I should go. Wait. Pants first, then go downstairs. Good choices.

"Where is everyone?"

"I didn't mean that they were precisely inside the house just yet. Moreso that they were on their way here and I could see them. They should be at the door momentarily...and then we can start."

We deal with our emotions differently. I become immobilized by the crushing weight of reality to the point that I can barely remember to put on pants. Ari channels all of her nervous energy into playing games. I can't blame her. The silly games we played as a family were the happiest times she ever knew. She used those moments of joy to distract herself from the wicked world around her. Maybe I should learn to be more like her. Maybe everyone should learn to be a little more like Ari.

David and Amera come in first. Salvo follows at a slightly slower pace. He uses a cane, but it appears to me now more an explanation of why he might travel slowly as opposed to a tool to help with a physical need. Maybe he just likes the distinguished look of a cane. He wields it well, and it fits with his overall mad scientist aesthetic—gray tufts of hair sprouting in every direction. Despite his age I'd still bet on him in a fist fight, that is, if someone managed to get past the blunt end of his cane.

"Welcome, and thank you for coming this morning. We are grateful for your help."

"No need for that now," Salvo quips, referring to my use of sign. "I can read lips, and dollars to donuts, I bet the girl can too." He turns to Ari with a smirk and a wink. "No one need sign on our behalf. You're all quicker with your lips."

Ari is delighted, bouncing up and down, clapping her hands. "I knew he'd be good at this game, Eli," she blurts out, "and we haven't even told him how to play yet!"

"Heavens, girl! I said you could read lips. I hadn't a clue that you could speak!"

Ari clasps her hand over her mouth in shock. Sheepishly, she removes it. "I guess I'm not a very good master of ceremonies, letting secrets fly before their time."

David and Amera are both confused. Salvo is happy; whether he understands or not, I can't tell.

"Let's sit. Ari, I think we should make sure everyone is caught up on what is going on."

Ari nods excitedly. She instinctively pulls out a chair at the end of the table for Salvo and then sits right next to him. She has a new friend.

"It's time for games," Ari announces. "They've already begun, but you haven't known the rules, of which there are very few; but it will help if you understand them and I'm certain you'll like it because it's a very fun game and we're going to have a lot of fun and you'll get to learn so many things about us and I can't wait for it to start."

"Should I paraphrase?" Both Amera and David look desperate for an explanation. Ari just shrugs her shoulders. Salvo waits with a grin on his face. I should paraphrase. "Ari helps me remember to appreciate the little things in life. Obviously, this is not a happy occasion for us. My parents, who are Ari's family as well, have been taken and we are distraught. We must accomplish something impossible; and when we do, we have more impossible tasks in front of us. We have no idea where my parents are and how to free them, and it is likely that our actions could have negative impacts on them. All of this is overwhelming, to the point that it is difficult to make it through a single day. So, we compartmentalize. I set aside all the impossibilities and everything that could go wrong. Then I acknowledge where I am and who I am with. I am safe, I am fed, and I am in the company of wonderful people. Thank you, again, for your hospitality. It is the diversions of life that keep us sane, that help us attain the impossible. So today, as we welcome a new friend into our temporary home, we intend to play a little game as a way of getting to know each other."

"I liked her version better," Salvo grins.

Game on.

"So how is this game played?" David asks.

"It's fairly simple; and really, it's mostly a game for Salvo, since we have shared a number of things with you and Amera already." Ari turns to look directly at Salvo. "You make wild guesses about us, and we tell you if you're right or not. You get to learn about us, and we get to learn how you think and how perceptive you are."

"It sounds like an excellent game," Salvo replies. "So, am I right about my first guess; or do I need to phrase it in the form of a question?"

"You mean *dollars to donuts*?"

"That's the one, my boy!"

"You are correct. I know the meaning of *dollars to donuts* because I am an August Child. How did you know? And where did you learn *dollars to donuts*? I mean, some idioms transfer; but that's not intelligible in the least."

"I had an inkling last night when I asked you to put out the fire, and you did not disappoint. You don't have to be of August to shift the wind, but your skill is beyond any I've seen. As for where I learned the phrase, I'm an old man and I have had many old friends. One of those many worked in Suvault and had learned a few curious phrases. He shared them with me, and I tucked them away for such a time as this."

If David and Amera are surprised at my shifting the wind, they don't show it on their faces.

"Tell us something else, wise man." If Salvo can't read Ari's sarcastic tone from her lips, he can definitely see it in the rest of her body. She oversells it on purpose. It's funny to watch, even making Amera smile.

"Young lady, would you please close your eyes for a moment?" Ari shuts them tightly and waits with great excitement. Salvo turns to me. "Speak to me a lie that she could not endure."

"Intellectually speaking, I have always been Ari's superior."

Ari doesn't need her eyes open to smack me on my shoulder. It makes everyone laugh. The test is obviously over, so she opens her eyes wider than I imagined possible. "What did you learn?" Childlike wonder fills her entire face. I will never get over that face.

"You act like you can hear," Salvo postulates. "You cannot hear, but you act like you can."

This is one of the most accurate things I have ever heard. So accurate, in fact, that Ari feels no need to expound further.

"One more?" She is a puppy, dropping a ball at the feet of her owner.

"Yes, one more." Salvo pauses. "I don't understand this one, so I'll just tell you what I have seen." He turns to the side, looking at us suspiciously through the slits of his eyes. A single eyebrow raises and a long dramatic pause serves the theatrical nature of this event.

"Last night," he begins tentatively, "one of you would repeat your story to the crowd while the other faced the elders. This was kind and endeared you to the people here. It also showed how connected the two of you are. Neither of you were overly focused on what the other had to say. You just knew. It's not even that you were each telling the same story with your own words. You knew how the other would tell the story and chose their words, though sometimes Ari would break rank if she thought your words were…"

"Dumb? Yes, I'm aware of her tendency to do that."

Salvo cracks a smile. "All very impressive," he continues, "but that's not what I am curious about. When the elders were speaking, sometimes it was more convenient for one of you to continue facing the crowd. You would turn if we spoke for long, but if our words were short you would remain fixed to the crowd. This did not bother me, but I noticed that you seemed to know everything that was said, whether facing us or turned away. How?"

"Turn, turn, turn, turn, turn!"

I was already turning before Ari said anything. I know exactly how this is going to go.

"Salvo," Ari begins eagerly, "would you agree that Eli is turned away from you and cannot see you?"

"Yes."

"Hold up any number of fingers you desire." She says.

He holds up four fingers. I do the same. He tries two. I copy. Seven: two on the right, five on the left. I mimic it exactly.

Now it's time for magic, or at least an educated guess to possibly finish him off. The square root of four is two. Four and two were the first two numbers. Seven, split between two hands, could be understood as twenty-five. It could also just be seven, but a perfect square is my only shot at greatness in this little game. I'll follow his limited pattern; one hand, five fingers—the square root of twenty-five. Now whip around for dramatic effect.

Salvo is laughing so hard he can barely catch his breath. "You're a clever boy! It's true that I was going to pick five next." He is still laughing, but hands don't require a full breath of air. "Now, the first three, how did you do it? Do you have eyes in the back of your head? Sometimes young children think this of their parents, but I've never known it to actually be true."

"Are you aware of video implants for those who are losing their eyesight?"

"I've heard of them," he admits, "but I've also heard they're quite costly."

"Well, the implants aren't too expensive. It's the program that goes with them that is expensive. My father came across a couple pairs of the implants without any program, so he picked them up cheaply. Luckily for us, we are very good at writing programs. The implants are installed on the back side of our ears. We have two small screens within our CI that show us exactly what's going on behind us."

"Fascinating! In all my days, I've not met anyone as interesting as the two of you, and I don't expect to meet your counterparts any time soon. Now, would it be admissible if I asked you a question?"

We nod in unison.

"Before Saree passed on, she talked about the need for another wind walker. People would believe a wind walker.

Your skills with the fire were impressive." He hesitates. "Can either of you walk on the wind?"

"No. What I did for you last night was more or less the extent of it. We have practiced some other motions that result in different things, but none of them have the force to bring us off the ground."

Salvo shakes his head slightly. "I thought not, but had to be sure." He pauses thoughtfully. "Are you familiar with the story of *The Boy and the Wind*?"

"Not I. Ari?"

She shakes her head.

"May I tell it to you?"

"Yes," we say in unison.

Salvo smiles, then begins. Just as before, the world fades away and all that is left is the story.

A young boy lived on a small island all by himself. He loved his life. He slept in a hammock every night, swinging back and forth to his heart's content. Every day he played in the sun. He learned to catch fish and he learned to make fire. In the evenings, he would sit by the fire, cook his food, and consider how lucky he was to have this wonderful life on this little island. Year after year he did the same exact thing each and every day until one day he stopped. It struck him that he had no friends on the island. His life here was too perfect to live alone. He had to share it with someone else. His mind was made up. He would travel to another land to find someone who would be his friend and share this perfect life with him. The following morning he got to work on building a raft out of driftwood that had washed up on the shore. Then he made a sail by weaving some leaves together. He gathered the few possessions he had and left.

The ocean was unforgiving. The waves crashed down on him, trying to tear his creation apart; but he soldiered on. The sun burned his skin and dried him out, leaving him thirsty and weak; but he soldiered on. The rain bore into his skin night after night, relentlessly striking him over and over; but he soldiered on. Eventually, he found a new land with marvelous trees and a city renowned for its ability to work with the wood: Euteka. The leader of Euteka came to meet with the boy and hear his story. The boy recounted all of his trials in reaching the city and his desire to find a friend to take back to his island. The leader refused the boy, telling him the residents would be terrified just by the telling of his story, let alone an invitation to return with him. The boy was sad, but determined to travel to another city where he might find a friend.

"Good sir," he asked the leader of the city, "why do you find my story so frightening? I would very much like to find a friend somewhere and I don't want to scare anybody. Maybe your advice could help me present my story in a better way to someone else."

The leader was impressed with the boy's polite resolve. He would help him before sending him off. "It's the wind. The wind of the day rips at your dry skin. The wind of the night pelts your body with rain and sleet. It is the wind that lifts the waves above your head and crashes them down on you. And the worst part is that you cannot see this enemy. He could attack you from anywhere at any moment. This, my boy, is why your story is too frightening."

The boy considered the leader's words carefully. He had been scared on his trip, but not because of the wind. "Sir, I think you are mistaken. I see the wind...not as a part of the night or the day, but in the color that stands between them; and I see him as my friend. He was my companion when I was all alone. He called to me and told me to face the fearsome ocean. He promised to stand by my side. He carried me through the storm and through the heat. He brought me to this new land. The wind was never my problem. He is the only reason I stand here today. He is the best friend I have ever known."

With that, the boy realized he did not need to find a new friend. He already had one. He thanked the leader for his help in discovering this, and they parted on good terms. The boy returned to his raft and sailed with the wind back to his island. Together, they spent the remainder of their days sharing every moment with each other. Never has there been a greater bond of friendship than that of the boy and the wind.

“Now tell me, have you seen the wind?” Salvo asks as if he knows the answer already.

Wide eyed, both Ari and I nod. We haven't discussed the void for years. It seemed fruitless without anything to guide us further, but we both remember it—the light in the distance—the color that stands between night and day. We both saw it. What does he know?

“You’re saying that the wind is what Ari and I saw in the void?”

“I cannot tell you what you have seen with your own eyes, but I do remember this: as a young boy, when this story was first told to me, I asked if anyone else had ever seen the wind aside from this lone boy. My mother recounted that Saree had once called the wind her friend and a constant companion. There is no written history of this, only what we have passed on through the ages; but the story of *The Boy and the Wind* is even older than Saree. She would have learned it growing up. She also would have known that calling the wind her friend would elicit comparisons to this story. I can think of no other reason for her to have said such a thing. Now remember,” he leans in, “many people can recall the void. Precious few have seen the wind.”

I want to know more. I want to ask him a million questions. I want...so very many things, but we don’t have time for that today. “Thank you for the story. I could spend ages considering every part of it and the meaning I might find for myself in it, but Ari and I have taken enough of your time already. We should discuss the reason we have gathered here today.”

David nods in agreement. “Yes, thank you both for the entertainment. It was delightful. And Salvo, thank you for the story.” He turns back to Ari and me. “The elders gathered this morning to discuss your situation further. We still gladly extend the same invitation we offered you last night, but I'm afraid we have nothing to offer you beyond that. Despite your formidable skillset, we do not see any way for you to be successful in your endeavors; and we cannot condone sending two young adults off to be captured and possibly tortured or killed by the Patricians. We see a fit for you here. We would like you to be a permanent part of our village."

This isn't a discussion. That's why everyone wasn't bothered by games and long stories...they wanted to let us down easy. My heart feels heavy.

"But what about Eunice and Isaac?" Ari stares blankly at David.

"It's unfortunate that they were taken, and I'm very sorry; but we have no way of knowing where they are or what is being done with them. I understand that you're grasping for anything that could bring them back to you, but we have felt for years that they are a bit foolhardy."

"And why is that?" My voice is distant—disconnected from me.

"Look," David postures, "your parents are very well-intentioned people, and their goals often align with ours; but they put themselves in dangerous positions. I am actually surprised that something like this didn't happen sooner."

"But they helped you," Ari says, disgusted. "Why can't you help them now?"

"It's not that simple, Ari. We have our people to think about. We can't handle being oppressed any further."

"And you already convinced the Patricians that we beat people bloody!" Amera spits out. "You don't think before you act; and you confirmed to those two men that we are just as savage as they already believed, if not more. I can't believe the-"

"Amera, that's enough." David gives her a sharp look.

"So you're not going to help us rescue my parents?"

"No," David shakes his head, "I'm afraid not."

"And you're not going to tell anyone in Evanwood about your decision because they loved my parents and would disagree with you, right?" It's all coming together now.

"Eli, it would be very dangerous to tell people your secrets, and we can't tell them about our decision without your unique qualities being a part of that conversation."

This is not an explanation. It is a threat. Time for a new tactic. "Why did you tell us about the Hall of Records?"

David stops short for a moment, flustered. "I told you about the Hall of Records to help you understand the impossibility of the situation, not to try and give you some glimmer of hope. The fact that you didn't understand that actually makes me more concerned for your ability to make sound decisions."

Ari picks up right where I left off, though she sounds a little more condescending than I would venture. "Since we obviously didn't understand, would you be so kind as to explain to us why it is impossible? We wouldn't want to run off and do something dumb."

David sighs in exasperation. "Fine, but understand this: I am doing this as a kindness to you in repayment for what your parents have done for us in the past. I will not take so kindly in the future to being pressured in this way."

We both nod solemnly. The future doesn't matter; not without my parents.

"I have explained some of this already, but I will go over it in detail so as not to have to repeat myself a third time. Door codes, and knowledge of Earth, are required to make it to the highest levels of the Hall of Records. While I understand you have knowledge of Earth, giving you the necessary codes would require a substantial risk on our end with no perceivable benefit to us. First and foremost, I must protect my people. Second, you wouldn't even make it through the front door. They scan your ID. Ari's would send a red flag immediately and she would likely be dead by evening. And Eli, I'm certain that you are on a watch list by now too. At a minimum, they would bring you in for questioning. At worst...the same fate as Ari. Lastly, accessing the information you need will raise a few flags. Not immediately, but after a few minutes there will be guards that come to check on the activity. Getting into the room is a death sentence in its own right. There would be no escape. Maybe you find the information you need, but you can't get that information out. There's just no way."

"Are there windows in every room?" Ari probes.

"I'm sure there are. We would have to check the schematics, but I don't see what that has to do with anything."

I feel my pulse quicken. This is our only gambit. "If we could prove to you that we can deal with all the issues you have brought up, will you consider helping us?"

"Even still, there is nothing to be gained. I love your parents; but they created this situation, and it is not our responsibility to get them out of it. Nor should they burden you with the task."

Here's the trump card; at least I hope it's the trump card. I take a half glance at Salvo and imagine I see the slightest nod. That's enough for me. "What if we could bring back the missing transcript from Saree and Bometir?"

"I could never condone such a mission," David postures.

"We wouldn't need you to condone it," Ari suggests. "We could do it against your wishes...if that was easier, of course."

David and Amera share a look with each other. Amera nods.

"Let's say someone were to give you the information you'd need." David is choosing his words carefully. "I could find myself in trouble if you did not return by...say...sundown, and I didn't report your absence to the Patricians."

"On a given day we could be certain to return by sundown. Ari?"

Ari nods.

"And if you never return?"

"I imagine the announcement would go something like this: Elias and Arielle left of their own accord, against my personal recommendation and in defiance of the elders."

"And if we do return," Ari smiles, "you can take all the credit for sending us on such a brilliant mission...if you want. I'm sure the people here would laud your accomplishment."

"And you understand the Order can't know about this until after the fact," Amera interjects, "right? We cannot say anything to them until the outcome is known. There's too much risk involved otherwise."

We are being manipulated, but this is our only chance. We both nod in agreement.

"Additionally," Amera continues, "we would find ourselves in a difficult position if you happened to be more self-serving than you have let on and return without the transcript from Saree and Bometir, or at least proof that it does not exist. Your insubordination, in that case, would have to be held up as an example—one with severe consequences."

"We have nowhere else to go." That's a lie; we could hide in the forest. "We are enemies of the Patricians." At least that part is true. "We will not allow anything to happen that would jeopardize our relationship with the Silent Order." Eh, mostly true on that last part.

"Great," David says casually. "Go ahead and convince us that you can deal with all the issues we have presented."

***

David rises from the table and stretches; it has been a tense hour of explanations. "Well, you have satisfied our concerns. I believe it is worth the risk."

Yes, it's worth the risk, because there's none for you. We shoulder all of the risk. It's fine. I'll keep my mouth shut.

"Let's get together tonight," Amera says, smiling. It makes my skin crawl. "I need a little bit of time to prepare all the details you'll need."

Ari finds it within her to act statelier than I am able, so she responds on our behalf. "That sounds wonderful, Amera. Let us know when is convenient and we will be ready for you."

"You two go on," Salvo says to David and Amera. "I could use a little more entertainment in my life, and these two amuse me so."

As the door shuts behind David and Amera, Salvo leans back in his chair with a large sigh. "Not everyone here is like David and Amera, you know. They are good people, but sometimes they choose to do things in a manner that is unbecoming of their position."

"She would see us die before returning without the document she wants!" Ari retorts.

"That's because of that stunt you pulled with the Patricians the other day," Salvo laughs. "That got under her skin in a bad way. I'm not sure she'll ever like you. Clever though, what you did showing your bruises and all. I can't imagine anyone could have come up with a better plan. Amera has a young boy; half your age, maybe. It was painful for her to see how people treated him—how the Patricians would talk about him. This place is a sanctuary for the two of them. The Patricians already see us as savages, so you did no real harm by making up that story of yours. And honestly, your story was more believable because it confirmed what they already believed to be true. But Amera still feels the pain. It's not right of her to treat you so poorly, but I can understand where it's coming from."

"Well, let's hope we return with what she wants; Ari doesn't need any more bruises".

"Bruises?" Ari's eyebrows raise high on her forehead. "I'm more concerned about a beheading!"

"Oh, come now. Threats of violence from the Order are idle. The worst they could do is hand you over to the Patricians, but that would result in a lot of bad blood with the people here. They may understand why the elders wouldn't run a rescue mission for your parents, but they would never understand handing you over for no apparent reason. David may be right about the carelessness of your parents, but the people here love them. So while David and Amera may like to think that they have the upper hand, you hold the hearts of the people; and that should not be underestimated."

"I guess that's comforting to know." Is comforting the right word? "But Salvo, why did you tell us about the transcript between Bometir and Saree?"

"Because you lacked leverage," Salvo grins. "I was fairly sure they wouldn't help you with what you truly wanted—it's nice and all to offer you a place to stay, but that's not why you're here—so I gave you a leg up."

"More like a corner to be backed into," Ari says, still frustrated.

"Truly now," Salvo continues, "did you get what you wanted? Forget all the stipulations...are you not in a better position today than you were yesterday?"

Ari and I share a blank stare with each other. He's right.

"Good. I didn't take either of you for fools who would back down when faced with a pinch of adversity."

"Why not just advocate on our behalf?" Ari's asks.

"I hadn't the means to prove you were up to the task. Only you could do that. In truth, I wanted to see for myself that you could handle it as well. The big difference being that I assumed you were capable and only needed confirmation."

It is relieving to know that at least one person is on our side. "Did you know my parents?"

"Lovely people! I can't wait to see them again. Is it true what you told David and Amera? They made each of you counterfeit identification documents?"

"They made one for Ari, but not for me. It was a calculated overstep on my part to say I already had one; I'm assuming we can copy the program they wrote and change a few things for me."

"Ha!" he laughs out loud. "Good choice. Probably for the best. You should get to work though. They may want to see it later tonight."

"What is that monstrous noise?"

"You heard that?" Ari exclaims. "My stomach grumbles when I get hungry."

"Did it not show up in your CI?"

"It did." She hangs her head in dismay. "I just thought maybe it was a fluke. Sorry, I'm just really hungry." She pauses. "I should go get us food."

I crack a smile and nod.

"I'll be back. Don't start without me," she hollers, running out the door.

"I should be on my way as well," Salvo groans as he rises from his chair. "I wouldn't be much help with that program of yours. One last piece of our game from earlier though, if you'd indulge an old man..."

"Of course."

"A fool in love says nothing too soon."

"Even in the midst of everything?"

"Absolutely in the midst of everything."

***

"First, we need to remove any reference to your parents since they were originally listed as my caretakers," Ari says as we sift through the code of her fake identification.

"Agreed. That should be simple. I'm more worried about any passcodes we might need to use in the process of setting mine up. Can the same passcode be used again? Or will that be a red flag as soon as we are scanned?"

"I'm headed to that part in the code right now. This had better work." Ari looks over at me. "It's going to work, right?"

"We don't have another option.

"Eli," Ari shrieks, "look in the comments!"

/~ In case of emergency:

Stewart Valden Courso
Edward Jean Malant
Fresnin Hyak Beldid
Samuel Cardid Blanch

Sandria Salven Cantor
Efri Skylan Merrow
Christine Mandel Estavo
Julia Tryan Verdic

Keys:
A7M12#79347
B9QK7#81356
F6L79#21998

P2K64#61798
G5TD2#92870
G0MC0#97080
K8G84#88241
Q7H19#76924

Talk to us before using these. There is risk involved for all four of us, so we should all be aware of their need and use. If you are unable to talk to us and you feel it is necessary to use one of these, then things have not gone as planned. We are sorry. Use caution. Don't do anything TOO stupid. Your mother/Eunice doesn't think I should have said that last part. She actually smacked me in the head just now. The things I put up with. Anyhow, be safe. It's a dangerous world out there.
~/

I can hear his voice. I want to actually hear his voice again. "They have everything ready for us...how did they know?"

"They didn't. There are four new identities for each of us. They were just being thorough. I bet setting up nine identities wasn't any more difficult than setting up one. I think the Order may be right; your parents were reckless in some regards. But they were also prepared for almost everything—even if they couldn't see it coming."

"You realize that all we have to do now is copy their code and plug in basic information, right?"

"It's only going to take twenty minutes."

"It's. Only. Going. To take. Twenty. Minutes. I was ready to spend hours."

"I was worried we wouldn't be ready by tonight."

"Me too."

"Lucky."

"We can use a little luck."

"Eli—I need you to know—after we finish...I'm going to take a nap."

"A nap sounds so good right now. I'm exhausted. I wasn't going to say anything because we had work to do, but I am relieved."

"Same."

***

"They're here." I gently rub Ari's shoulder to wake her. She pops up from her bed and heads downstairs to open the door before I can. David, Amera and Salvo shuttle in. "I took a nap this afternoon," she says mid yawn, arms stretched out. "It felt so lovely."

"Why did no one tell me naps were in order for today?" Salvo scans the room accusingly.

David and Amera both chuckle. They seem to be in a better mood than this morning. That's good.

Ari is the last to find a seat at the table. "I believe we end with the Hall of Records. How do we begin?"

Amera slides a small metallic disc onto the table. "We have friends in Suvault who have given us this. Just tap it with your finger once and we'll all be looking at the same thing."

With a simple touch, a three-dimensional schematic of the Hall of Records hangs in the air in front of me.

"Everyone gets a CI at one month old," David explains, "but members of the Silent Order are severely restricted in what they can access."

"But neither of you were born deaf," Ari stresses.

"Access to your CI is handicapped when you join the Order, deaf or not. Not to worry, it doesn't affect us much in our day to day lives. And we've created some workarounds, anyhow. The disc, in this case, holds all the information and constantly runs a program trying to connect to a display. The feed escapes through any path it can and displays the image you see before you. Certainly, your CI was limited at birth," he says, looking at Ari, "but I imagine you have since been given full access."

She nods with a quiet smirk.

I don't want to hear David's opinion on whether or not Ari *should* have full access or not. "So your screen functions, but your programs are limited. The disc runs the program for you and uses your empty screen." This is an impressive workaround.

"Precisely," Amera beams. Is she actually chipper this evening? "Now let's discuss what's before us: The Hall of Records. Anyone can enter the main floor of the building at the south entrance. You'll have to register upon entry, but you have that covered with your forged documents?"

We both nod.

"Good," she continues. "General information is accessible on the main floor, but what you need is on the seventeenth floor—the highest level of the building. If you enter the staircase located in the Northeast corner you will only have five checkpoints to get through. This was the simplest path we could find. Other paths might be shorter in distance, but they have more checkpoints."

Amera is staring directly at us as if she has asked us a question. Fine, I'll play your game. "That sounds prudent. Walking a little further is no trouble."

Satisfied, she continues, "At each checkpoint you will need an access code and to answer a question related to Earth. We have taken care of the access codes. If you touch any checkpoint on the display you can see the access code. Another reason we want to limit checkpoints is because we assume your knowledge of earth is not comprehensive. If you don't know an answer to something you'll have to pick another route. If you place an X on a checkpoint, like so," she uses her finger to draw on the display at the first checkpoint, "you'll see a new path with the fewest checkpoints possible. Each checkpoint will have a different question. The questions are open ended. You can speak an answer and it will be analyzed. No need to be exactly precise in how you present the answer, but please understand, if you answer a question incorrectly it will send out an alert. One alert by itself may not inspire anyone to check out the situation, but multiple alerts will."

"So all we have to do is sneak through the maze of people who would want to kill us if they knew who we were, answer some questions almost no one knows the answer to, get into the room we need, hack their system, pull the appropriate files, and then escape without being seen. Does that sound about right?"

Amera gives a healthy grin at my summation. "Well, I hadn't gotten to the part about hacking their system yet, but yes, you'll need to do that too."

"Will that set off an alarm?"

"It seems likely, but I've never known of anyone who tried it. It's a rather stupid idea." Her smile morphs into a grimace. "If you trigger an alarm—and let's assume you will—you'll have three minutes, at most, before someone arrives; and I would not recommend being there when they do."

Three hours making plans, covering every detail, and we are done.

"Ari and I will leave in the morning. We will return by sundown the day of my birthday."

"It's a good plan," David nods.

The stillness in the room is palpable. Everyone is a little nervous.

"As this is my last night for a while with a comfortable bed," Ari announces, "I'm going to sleep."

With that, everyone leaves. We are alone.

"It's going to work, right?" Ari's eyes share the same hopeless feeling I have.

"It has to."

CHAPTER 15
PARADISE

It's been Eleven days since we arrived in Paradise. It's the same thing every day. Breakfast in the morning, then forty kilometers of new flight paths. It's a little under 200 kilometers from here to Suvault, but we need two separate paths and they don't exactly make straight lines. We return for lunch and then practice shifting. We do want to become better at it, but right now it serves as meditation. Deep breath. The motion is calming. All through the day—whenever we can talk—we discuss the details of our plan along with every contingency. I've memorized it twenty times over by now—Ari too—but repetition is the key to success in the face of alarming odds. But right now...this moment I use to ground myself in reality. My name is Elias Jameson Hall. My parents were taken from me by the Patricians and I have to get them back. I have to try. I have to do something. Breathe. Calm. Ari is with me. We are working together and we will succeed; the alternatives are not palatable. We must hide our identities or we will be killed—I will be Steward and Ari, Sandria. We must execute our plan flawlessly or we will be killed. Deep breath. It's going to work. It has to work.

"Break for dinner?" Ari says, breaking me out of my trance.

"Yes please. My mind is a little too focused on dying."

"You don't want to?"

"Die?"

"Yes."

"No."

"Good, me neither."

"Help me get my mind off it?"

"Certainly. Yesterday you said you needed to rest, not wanting to 'burn the candle at both ends.' Why would someone burn a candle at both ends?"

"That's just it, you see, the candle will burn up faster and then be of no use."

"I get that, but I still don't understand why someone would do it."

"No one does it. That's the point."

"If no one does it, how do people know what it means?"

"That is a really fair point. I guess people learn about this thing that doesn't happen in order to compare it to their own work ethic."

"That would make me think that someone who is *burning the candle at both ends* has no work ethic because it doesn't exist."

"It just means that you're overworking yourself."

"Why don't you just say that?"

"Because somehow it became more believable to compare yourself to a fictional act than to just say what you mean."

"I don't trust Earth."

"You don't trust an entire planet?"

"Not at all. It's very strange—shifty." Ari spits on the ground in mock disgust.

"Well I don't trust deaf girls who can speak clear as a bell. They're very strange and shifty as well."

"First of all, I have worked very hard on my image and am proud to be seen as strange and shifty! And second, why is a bell considered clear?"

"Honestly, I have no idea. It's just something people say."

"They certainly do not."

"Correction, it's something that people used to say on a different planet in a distant galaxy that is likely billions of light years away."

"I guess that will have to do. You really should learn to talk sometime, though. I did. It took a while, but I got the hang of it. You could too."

"I'll take it into consideration."

"Happy birthday, by the way!"

"You know it's not my birthday until tomorrow."

"I just thought I might be a little preoccupied tomorrow. You know, with trying to save the world and all. Figured I would get it in today for good measure."

"I do not accept."

"You don't accept my birthday well wishes?"

"No."

"I don't think that's something you can turn down. I gave them to you. No gives backsies."

"Too bad, I just gave them back."

"Well, if you gave them back it means you at least received them to begin with. That's good enough for me."

"I'm not going to win this one, am I?"

"Not in the least."

Ari lays her head on my shoulder. We sit in silence eating our food as twilight turns to darkness. One last night in paradise. I hope we get another.

***

The flight to Suvault feels like only a few minutes...my mind is wholly elsewhere. We both committed to reviewing the plan on our own while flying, but all I can think about are the words Salvo shared with me: *a fool in love says nothing too soon.*

We stop short of the throughway, standing several meters from the clearing. Everything after this moment could go terribly wrong. I didn't want to distract from our preparations, so I've said nothing. But now, before we step into a different world, I have to tell her. I turn towards Ari to speak and she kisses me. It isn't long, nor is it short. Now...the thing...there was...I was going to...I...brain, work!

"You're in love with me, right?" Ari says softly.

"Uh...of course."

"Good. I just wanted to make sure before we off ourselves by way of this terrible plan we have." She flits her eyes in opposite directions of each other—her 'crazy face'.

"Good thinking. You know I was just about to-"

"I know. I'm in love with you too." Her voice is sweet and reassuring.

I take her hand in mine. I will not let go...not for anything. We stand in silence taking everything in. A single breath in...out...and we step into the open.

"I've never seen anything like this before," Ari marvels. "So many buildings—so close together. It's unnatural."

"They must have teams of hundreds of people constantly editing the code in the trees to keep them in this state. I didn't expect things to be quite so busy. There's a lot of pods flying overhead."

"Live a little." Ari grips my hand tighter.

We approach the third building on the left. "This should be it." My heart is racing.

"I remember seeing the Children's Center at a month old. It felt out of place. This monstrosity wholly does not belong."

"It's modeled after skyscrapers from Earth. I knew that the first time I saw it on Amera's schematic, but seeing it in person..."

"I know."

Every step up to the main entrance brings more anxiety. Are we walking too fast? Too slow? Are my steps too loud? Do I look normal? Am I doing anything that might raise an alarm? We interface with the system at the main entrance and provide identification. I can't breathe. Green light. Ari too. At least it's not red. No one seems perturbed by our arrival. Keep moving.

Terminals line the walls and a smattering of people are logged in at various stations, searching public records. A single Patrician at a central station mans the floor. He's there to help. I doubt he can give us the help we need. *Walk to the terminal that is closest to the Northeast corner of the room.* It's good we spent so much time memorizing the plan. We pretend to work for ten minutes until we can see in our rear view that the Patrician is occupied with someone at the main desk. Calm, but swift, we move to the locked door a few feet away from our station; the first checkpoint. Ari types in the code and then we see our first question on the screen:

DESPITE OVERWHELMING SCIENTIFIC EVIDENCE TO THE CONTRARY, THERE IS AN OUTSPOKEN MINORITY THAT BELIEVE THE EARTH IS WHAT?

"Flat."

I hear the lock release. We're in. The hallway is long and we need to reach the far end. We move.

"People think the Earth is flat?" Ari signs so we can't be heard.

"Some people do."

"Do you?"

"Of course not!"

"I wouldn't love you any more if you did." She mock-spits.

"Well that's a relief." This is exactly what I need; just enough interaction to keep me from freaking out, and not so much I'm actually distracted.

"Seriously though, why would someone believe the Earth is flat?"

"They think it's a big conspiracy."

"What would be the point of convincing people the Earth is spherical when it is not?"

"I honestly have no idea. You'd have to ask a flat Earther."

"That's the worst designation I've ever heard!"

"Well, they aren't too bright to begin with, so it's not too surprising."

Ari's bemused smile matches mine. And then we're there: the entrance to the staircase. Ari puts in the code at the checkpoint, and then another question appears:

IN 1984, THE MINISTRY OF LOVE HELPS PEOPLE LEARN TO LOVE WHO?

"Big Brother." It's open.

"I'm not even going to ask. You don't make any sense at all."

"It's a novel. If it were written about Merced it would have been the Patricians that the ministry helps people love."

"Why would someone write such a disgusting thing?"

"It's satire. The author didn't mean it."

"How do you know the author didn't mean it? Did he tell you that?"

"No."

"Then I don't trust him."

"It's just fiction. Big Brother doesn't exist."

"Of course big brothers exist. You're speaking nonsense."

"You're not understanding it right. It's that–"

"Shhh. Someone might be coming."

Nobody is coming. "Did you just shush me? I'm signing."

"Shhh."

We walk in silence. *Make it to the highest floor, seventeen stories up. Two more checkpoints in the stairwell and one final one to reach the room.*

We make it to the sixteenth floor without seeing anybody. This is not a particularly quick route, but Amera was right to choose it. Most people use the elevators. Fine with me as long as we don't see anybody. The entrance to the floor—as well as the staircase going up—is blocked by another checkpoint. Ari puts in the code again. Another question. I do enjoy a good routine.

SPELL THE WORD "BINGO" FOR THE THIRD TIME.

clap *clap* "N-G-O." It's open.

I can tell Ari is furious with my answer, and the fact that it worked.

"We will discuss this when we get back," she signs like a parent rebuking a child.

We don't have time to discuss it any further right now. One more flight of stairs and we reach another door. Code first, then another question:

WHAT IS THE INTENDED MEANING OF THE PHRASE, "THANKS, EINSTEIN!"?

"You are an idiot." We're through.

The lobby we are in is small. No one else is around; they really trust their security measures. The center door is the one we need.

"Who was Einstein?" Ari asks as we traverse the room.

"One of the smartest people that ever lived on Earth."

She shakes her head with a look of dismay. "Earth people don't make sense." She puts in the code and our last question appears:

HOW MANY PEOPLE WERE EXECUTED IN THE SALEM WITCH TRIALS?

I don't know. We made it this far and I don't know. Everyone knows about the witch trials. I'm sure I've even seen documentaries on it, but I haven't a clue as to how many people were executed. I don't think it was in the hundreds, but beyond that I'm lost. I could guess, but I was hoping for more than a one percent chance of entering this room. I am frozen. My vision is closing in. This was a terrible idea. We never should have come. What are we going to do?

"Twenty."

No. She wouldn't. Why? We made it all this way. We only had one shot at this. Why would she guess without even discussing it with me?

"I know things too." She smiles at me as the door opens. "Mulfer talked about the witch trials in *The Knowledge of The Possible*. You didn't know the answer. I've seen that face before. So I answered as quick as I could in case you decided to blurt out some stupid guess. I mean, after clapping to spell BINGO, I didn't want to see what you would come up with next."

I don't have time for all the emotions I feel. Get over it, Eli. There are larger things at stake. Ari shuts the door behind us as we step in the room. It isn't very large, maybe five meters on each side. The far wall opens to a balcony overlooking the throughway below. Had we more time, it would be a great view to enjoy. To either side of the balcony opening is a console and a chair. Logging in to the system is simple enough. One additional code for each of us and we both have a connection. Now we just have to search, and quickly.

"Don't forget to set your timer."

"Thanks." I *think* I would have remembered. "Three minutes and counting. Recite the roles." I'm still a little shaken. This helps.

"I will find anything I can related to Isaac and Eunice. You look for the rest of *The Silence of Saree.* Search terms and results will be spoken aloud. Whoever finishes their job first can join the other. If one minute remains and we have not found either we will both search for Isaac and Eunice; finding them is our primary goal. We'll deal with the consequences later."

"Saree Octavien Saldred. 8,000 results."

There's no convenient way to filter results. We have to search a new term every time. I can't read 8,000 titles in three minutes. Next search term it is.

"Eunice Saric Hall. 1,200 results."

Too many for Ari as well. Don't stress; we expected this. Everything is going to be fine.

"Alfred Hugo Bometir. 5,000 results."

"Isaac Canter Jameson. 1,200 results."

"Bometir Saree. 3,000 results." None of this is any surprise. It's just due diligence.

"Hall arrest. Jameson Arrest. Both searches, zero results."

"The Silence of Saree. 4,000 results."

"Elias Jameson Hall. One result. File transfer."

File transfers could take up to fifteen seconds. That's what Amera said. We only have time to download a few documents. At least we have one.

"This is the history that is known. 82 results. I'm scanning through titles."

"Ariell Linivette SO. One result. File Transfer."

"Title: Silencing Saree. Read it!"

Fifteen seconds allotted to reading pertinent titles. I start at the top. Ari starts half way down. Either one of us can call for a file transfer at any point before the time is up.

Ari screams! What is it? What's wrong?

"Saree wasn't of August! She was like me!"

"Silencing Saree. File transfer. One minute left."

"Stedny arrests. Zero results. Eli, we're out of search terms."

"Try Romeo and Juliet." Father was playing Romeo the day he left...it's better than nothing.

"Romeo and Juliet. Five results."

"There's people outside the door. I can hear them. At least four, maybe more."

"First result, no."

"They put in the code, Ari. Hurry! My file transfer is done I'm logged off. I'll do what I can to hold them off."

"Second result. No."

"We only have one shot at this to find my parents!"

"Shut up! Let me work! Third result. Hall Jameson referenced! File transfer!"

The door swings open towards Ari, keeping her hidden from view. I wait a single second to let one of the Patricians enter the doorway before shifting with all my might. The gust slams the door into the Patrician, knocking him back, creating a domino effect with the rest. Perfect!

"The door is shut. They didn't see either one of us. They'll have to put the codes in again. We should be gone before it opens. Ten seconds if we're lucky."

"Done!" Ari leaps out of her seat and we both run to the balcony. She locks eyes with me. This will be our last moment together. "At least a balcony is better than a window." She smiles at me. "See you in Paradise." And with that, she jumps over the edge. The door swings open, but I am already on my way, following Ari. I doubt any of them will follow me.

Terminal velocity isn't quite as fast on Merced as it is on Earth—the gravitational pull here isn't quite as high. But that doesn't really matter considering that the difference is negligible and the height I jumped from—though not actually enough to reach terminal velocity—is certainly high enough to kill me. Why am I thinking of this now? What is wrong with me? Evidently my stupid brain is set on occupying me with trivial things before I die. How lovely.

Focus. Calm down. Our flight paths are built on the same concept as the throughways. Our suits should allow us to fly on the throughways as well as the paths we have made for ourselves. We have a very strong theory involving scientific reasoning that would suggest the throughway will catch us, so to speak. Pods float at ten meters off the ground. That means we have ten meters to be caught by this invisible field. Please let the science be right...please let the science be right.

As I enter the field of the throughway the pressure against my chest forces out all the air I have. I can't breathe! The ground is getting close! I'm slowing. Slowing. Still three meters off the ground and I begin to rise. I didn't die! This is a fantastic moment to be me! Except that I'm going very, very fast—faster than any of the pods. My vertical speed has been translated into horizontal speed. This isn't especially helpful since we are flying into oncoming traffic, but at least it will get us out of here quickly.

A pod is coming directly at me. This is why we made the button; *press and hold the button on your chest and the suit loses connection with the throughway*. That's what Ari had suggested. I fall and the pod passes over me. Releasing the button, I float up to ten meters again. This isn't frightening at all. Just another normal day almost dying at every moment. Focus. Ari is up ahead. Good. She veers off to take our first escape route. We are only allowed to take the same route if no one saw us. That's the rule. No one saw our faces, but they knew of our presence; so I do not follow her. An extra hundred meters and I'm at the next escape route. I veer off into the trees. No one is behind me. No one noticed us aside from the Patricians on the top floor and possibly a few frightened people in the pods we dodged. No one saw where we went; but even if they did, Mother's getaway loop will destroy all of our code ten minutes after use. We've done it—we made it out alive!

My speed has normalized. I feel safer traveling at a lower speed. Still, every muscle in my body is tense. I need to relax. It's going to be a few hours of flying until I meet up with Ari. But it's ok; it all worked. I can't believe it worked!

***

I approach the clearing from the South. Ari would have come in from the East. I half expected her to be here waiting for me, but she is also one for theatrics and probably wants to meet in the clearing. That will be better. She should have only arrived a few minutes before me, so it might be a bit much for her to reach me already. I'm tired of being still, and I want to see Ari now. Running, therefore, is my best option...and it feels good. Besides, Ari may not know it, but slow motion theatrical runs are about as epic as things get; and my Ari deserves nothing less.

I should be able to see her from the edge of the clearing. She's running too. Perfect! No. She's running from! Eight Patricians are chasing after her along the edge of the ravine. They trip her and surround her almost instantly. Go faster, Eli. I'm 200 meters away. Ari raises her right hand as high as she can, makes a full rotation with her entire body and then slams her hand into the ground. Every one of the Patricians is knocked over. Good job Ari! 150 meters. She runs, but one of the Patricians grabs her by the ankle. She falls. The others have risen and are surrounding her again. They're screaming profanities at her. 100 meters. Faster. They stand her up, her back to the ravine. The circle shrinks around her as they draw in closer. 50 meters. The man closest to Ari looks back and sees me. Staring into my eyes, he smirks and shoves Ari's shoulder. She's falling backwards. 10 meters. There are no trees below, no water, no safety of any kind. I shift. Every ounce of energy I have pushes behind me. Breaking through the line of Patricians, I dive off the edge of the ravine.

This is the second time today that I have followed Ari off a great height. The difference, however, is stark. The first time I intended to live. This time, I do not. There are very few things that I am sure of in this life, but one of those is Arielle Linivette SO. I will not live without her. In the last two weeks we have discussed at great length what we think will happen when we die. It was a bit morbid considering we both knew it was a real possibility today, but it also helped clear our minds and gave us something interesting to think about. Our best assumption was that, upon death, we will travel somewhere new and begin again. It's unlikely that we will remember anything about this life, though my odds seem slightly higher than hers. One evening we even made a silly pact; if we are to die together we should hold hands, allowing for the possibility that we might travel together through the void and find each other again. There is no scientific basis for this assumption; and we agreed that the idea, in and of itself, was stupid. But it is the only thing in my mind—my only hope. Better together than apart. This world treated us poorly anyhow. Maybe the next will be kinder.

Ari is falling backwards. She is looking up at me as I dive towards her with all my might. I know she'll be angry that I followed her, but she must be resigned to the fact that I cannot change the decision I made, so she is reaching for me just the same that I am reaching for her. Our hands connect. In that single moment, we both realize exactly what is going to happen. Early on we tried shifting while touching each other, but we were both very poor at it and the results were abysmal. We tried it every few years, and though we did improve, it was always disjointed and awkward. We always competed against each other; even when working together, it was a competition. But in this moment, we are of one mind. The adrenaline coursing through my body helps me feel it—the charge. I spent everything I had only moments ago in an attempt to reach

Ari, but I now have more. Not just more. Now, an insurmountable power flows through me—flows through us. A few meters from the ground and we shift. I create a giant cloud of dust by applying my force to the ground so it looks as though we meet our end. At the same time, Ari stops us. We stand, hidden in the cloud, not touching the ground. We look at each other, faces filled with shock, wonder, terror and amazement. This is everything we have been working for. This is everything we need. This will change *everything*. We are wind walkers.

Made in the USA
Columbia, SC
29 October 2020

23587381R00139